'What's most striking about *Marlo* is its quiet dignity, the lightness of touch with which Carmichael tells this story, which is about recognition and discovery as much as it is about love. Christopher's unfolding realisation, that in order to come of age he must also cast himself out, is never cause for him to abandon his optimism and his willingness to hope for and work for a life and a love, however unsanctioned, of his own making. Carmichael's reclaiming of a sidelined history is defiantly hopeful too, resisting tragedy and seeking out forgotten joys instead.'

FIONA WRIGHT, author of *Small Acts of Disappearance*

'Falling in love can be terrifying and all the harder when the laws of the land are against you. *Marlo* is a deeply affecting novel; tender and brutal by turn.'

SOPHIE CUNNINGHAM

PRAISE FOR *IRONBARK*

'Jay Carmichael's *Ironbark* does the extraordinary.
It achieves what we readers want from the best of
fiction: to tell a story anew, and to capture a world
in all its wonder, ugliness, tenderness, and cruelty.
This is a novel of coming of age and of grief that
astonishes us by its wisdom and by its compassion.
It's a work of great and simple beauty, so good it
made me jealous. And grateful.'

CHRISTOS TSIOLKAS

'[An] accomplished debut ... Carmichael has a poetic
turn of phrase, and he plays with time, moving the
story back and forth ... keeping readers on their toes.'

BOOKS+PUBLISHING

'What *Ironbark* captures beautifully is the yearning
one might feel while growing up unable to understand
or express love and attraction freely; a yearning to kiss
your best friend, a longing for an end to a loneliness,
like cracked land waiting for rain. *Ironbark* is a still,
quiet, compelling novel that reaches an ending both
sad and peaceful.'

GOOD READING

'The novel draws deeply on the love of nature that
once inspired Carmichael to pursue botanical science
... It is almost poetic in its descriptions of a slightly
surreal landscape overcome by an oncoming storm
that seems to mirror Markus's silent struggles.'

SBS.COM.AU

'While it feels like a cliché to call a novel — especially
one by a first-time author — "assured", it is the phrase
I kept returning to while reading this debut offering
… [Carmichael's] clean and polished prose possesses
the kind of confidence that puts readers at ease …
Ironbark is a poised and atmospheric work that
reveals Carmichael as an author to watch.'

READINGS

'[A] subtle, impressionistic novel about adolescent
alienation and masculinity in rural Australia …
Carmichael paints an exquisitely tender portrait
of doomed adolescent longing and love.'

THE MONTHLY

'*Ironbark* is an elegant novel, one that reveals itself
slowly. It is both a wonderful evocation of the
listlessness of grief and a disturbing portrait of shame
and self-doubt. In many ways the story is as familiar
as the town, hot and dusty with drought, but it is also
fresh and new, as it questions with an unexpected
urgency what it means to be a man.'

ADELAIDE ADVERTISER

'It is convincing as the voice of a young man full of
longing, awkwardness, and a passion for things he
will no doubt soon grow out of … *Ironbark* is a book
about being stuck: the story does not develop so
much as deepen.'

WEEKEND AUSTRALIAN

MARLO

Jay Carmichael is a writer and editor whose first novel, *Ironbark*, was shortlisted for the Victorian Premier's Literary Award for Fiction in 2019, and whose writing has been published by Beyond Blue and appeared widely in print and online, including in *Overland*, *The Guardian*, SBS, and The Telling Tree project. Jay lives and works in Melbourne.

MARLO

JAY CARMICHAEL

SCRIBE

Melbourne • London

Scribe Publications
2 John St, Clerkenwell, London, WC1N 2ES, United Kingdom
18–20 Edward St, Brunswick, Victoria 3056, Australia
3754 Pleasant Ave, Suite 100, Minneapolis, Minnesota 55409, USA

Published by Scribe in Australia and New Zealand 2022
Published by Scribe in the United Kingdom and North America 2023

Typeset in Caslon by the publishers

Internal pages designed by Laura Thomas

Printed and bound in the UK by CPI Group (UK) Ltd, Croydon CR0 4YY

Scribe is committed to the sustainable use of natural resources and
the use of paper products made responsibly from those resources.

978 1 911344 20 9 (UK edition)
978 1 925713 69 5 (Australian edition)
978 1 957363 09 7 (US edition)
978 1 922586 55 1 (ebook)

Catalogue records for this book are available from the
National Library of Australia and the British Library.

scribepublications.co.uk
scribepublications.com.au
scribepublications.com

For Ma

Any male person who in public or in
private commits or is a party to the
commission of or procures or attempts
to procure the commission by any male
person of any act of gross indecency with
another male person shall be guilty of
a misdemeanour and shall be liable to
imprisonment for a term of not more
than three years.

Crimes Act 1949

I held the payphone receiver close to my mouth. The
train station was a cavernous, domed echo chamber. It
had taken what felt like a day to arrive in Melbourne and
for most of the journey I'd been asleep. I also held the
receiver close, almost against my lips, because it brought
me closer to my sister, Iris, who was the only person I
spoke to when I arrived at my destination. She was faint
through the phone.

'Thanks for organising a place for me to stay,' I said.

'When you're settled,' she said, 'I'll visit.'

A teeming street, rows of cars, through the glass of

the phone box. Grey smog. I fiddled with the front of my shirt. Sighed.

'Yes. Come down, have a picnic with me,' I said, adding, 'when I'm settled.'

'When will that be?'

My fingers wrapped round the phone cord. 'I'll let you know.' I don't recall saying goodbye or if she did. She had been in contact with an old school friend of ours. He'd moved away from our home town, Marlo, a few years before I left. I was meeting him now. Seeing a man about a dog and whatnot.

I made my way out of the station and onto the street. A fidgety mass of people crossed what seemed to be an endless intersection. A barrage of arms and bags and feet and papers pushed me back onto the kerb, and I had to wait for the next cycle of human movement to cross. I fell in behind a taller man who slipped between the crowd and was headed in the same direction as I was. Once we reached the other side, he continued on with the flow while I entered a three-storey pub on the corner. It was quieter inside, but I doubted there were any fewer people in there than outside. I took my travel case up the stairs and ordered a pint of dark ale. I sat in a luxurious armchair beside a window, looking down onto the intersection I'd navigated minutes before. Another flow, seaming, slicing, as if mimicking the river only a few hundred yards down the road.

I regarded the room. Men. Dressed in tailored suits,

ties ironed, collars starched. My own outfit betrayed me as an outsider. I had come from quiet pastures that smelled of grassy cow pats. I shrugged on my large overcoat and finished off the beer. What on earth would *you* do here? No home. No car. No pounds or shillings. No job. No friends. No family. Only this meeting with a man I'd not seen since I was a child. Few clothes, fewer underclothes. And the sky was getting darker. As I fished in my pocket for the coin I thought I had, getting ready to stand, a firm hand gripped my shoulder. A rather dashing man stood behind me; he laughed.

'Don't you remember?' He rested a hand on his chest near his clavicle. Broad-shouldered, blond hair, blue eyes: an advertisement for anything. A film star. James Dean.

I wanted to run my hand over him and verify his realness. I did not recognise him, but said, 'Of course. Kings.'

'Kings,' he chuffed.

Broad-shouldered, blond hair, blue eyes …

'Kings. Yes.'

'Mind, I got a bit more round me middle.' He patted his tummy.

I said, 'Hardly recognisable.'

He took this as a joke and an invitation. He sat in the spare armchair across from me. 'I'm so glad Iris got in touch.'

'Me, too. I don't know a soul here.'

He winked. 'You know one now.'

He shouted another round. When he came back

from the bar, I asked, 'What d'you do down here?'

He pointed to a bundle of suits behind us. 'Got a gig as a court reporter at the *Bulletin*.'

'That rag?'

'Better than working on the *Marlo Gazette*.' He laughed. 'And it pays the bills.' His blue-grey eyes landed on me. He half-smiled. 'I didn't think I'd be seeing you again.'

'You're living the life my sister has always wanted.'

'She come up with you?'

I shook my head. 'Back home. Much to her disgust.'

'Well,' he said, 'you'll have her to thank for being able to live that city-life, too.' He looked down at the travel case Iris had packed for me. 'Have you only just got here?'

I drew the case closer. Being the shorter of us, I couldn't help but feel as if he looked down on me. I wondered if he noticed that I spoke as he once had — clunky phrases, swallowed noises, cut-off words.

Perhaps this is what prompted him to say next, 'Long way to travel and not know what you're doing.'

'Yeah.'

'You got any plans for work?'

'Between jobs.'

'You come here for a bird?'

'God no.' I shook my head.

And then he laughed. 'Don't tell me you're running *away* from a bird.'

*

Kings and I used to play Aussie Rules at school. Boys versus girls. I'd stand with the group of boys out in the middle of the oval. Bodies, sweating, studded the paddock, barren, beside the old school building. Tough and rough boys, most boys. Not me: in that space, I was the final stem of greying wheat, ready to be scythed. A chorus chased a shiver down my back: *Footy!* That's what the older boys yelled in deeper tones. I stood behind Kings — my voice didn't dip as deep — somewhat near the edge of the group as the boys, flexing their biceps, yelled again: *Footy!* Kings often had his hands down the front of his shorts. Back then, he was tall and broad but skinny in his school kit. Mesmerising: his fingers under the material of his shorts, rolling like waves, scratching. We lived quite close to one another, with his family property just a bit further on down the road from ours. We had to cross a large paddock together to get us in the right direction. We ducked under the barbed-wire fence. I focused on not getting my good shirt caught in the wire; Ma'd kill me. Once inside the paddock, no trees protected us from the spiky sun.

Bombs broke through cathedral roofs and bullets tore through young men's chests. But not there, not in Marlo where we were. The theatres of war were distant — reports of them played out from Da's portable radio more like an evening drama. Except for the fallen who were closer, who were the little cut-out newspaper notices tacked up in the main street's shop windows.

'My cousin Jimmy's come to live with us,' I told him. 'His ma went troppo and sent him over. I have to share a room.'

Kings ran a hand over the tips of the crop and the longer weeds, which reached up above his navel. 'Lucky we're too young for war.'

'Jimmy wants to go,' I said. 'He sleeps with a toy soldier.'

'Where'd his ma go?'

I shrugged.

'When's she back?'

I shrugged.

Kings put a hand down the front of his trousers.

I asked him why he was scratching.

'My things.'

I'd never had to scratch my things. I looked down the front of myself, to my waistline. I said, 'Ma says if I put my hands anywhere near my things she'll take them off with a butcher's knife.'

'I got hairs growing,' he said, 'I can't help it.'

I laughed.

'True.'

'Bulldust.'

'I'll show you if you don't believe me.' His fingers scratched behind the material.

A hot, uncomfortable prickle slashed my brow. 'Nah.'

He stopped in the middle of the paddock, fingers at his fly. 'I'll show you.' And he did show. And, yes, there were hairs growing round his things.

At first, I wanted to touch his things and their hairs. But then a deep pang stunned my body and it told me: *recoil.* That was what was expected.

'Y'got them, too?' He re-buttoned.

I shook my head.

'Bet it's 'cause I got more,' he laughed.

The sun grew hotter.

'Show us.'

I had an urge to push Kings so the weeds and crop swallowed him. I ran away, swiping at the blades as if I were now the scythe. When I got home I pushed past Iris, who was in the hallway, and entered the bathroom. Locked the door. I pulled down my trousers and undies to reveal my own pink and smooth things. My huffing face, sweaty, stared back from the mirror.

It was this same feeling I had while sitting across from Kings at the pub, when he assumed my coming to the city was for a bird. What else would my ghost be doing there with only a travel case to my name? So small, so insignificant. No substance. If I went out into the street and stood in front of a passing car, I'd slide up and over the bonnet in a spectacular burst of dust. My response back then had been to run from him, because I hadn't understood how seeing his *things* had made me feel. While I didn't understand this default instinct of mine — the urge to disappear — I would not run this time. I would not run because I had nowhere to go.

Down the road and around the corner from Kings's place in Melbourne was a mechanic's garage. It had a tall frame, clad in corrugated iron, with a roller-door front. This was the first place I thought of when I considered finding work because I didn't know about much else. I walked into that place with my chest pushed up, though I expected to be laughed back out. A bloke, grease-stained in purple-blue overalls, stood inside and made a mark on a piece of paper he held. I followed him round the front of a car he must have been assessing. I told him I wanted work. He asked what use was I.

'I know my way around an engine.' I pointed out-wards, in what I believed was the direction of my father's property, way away in Marlo. 'I've worked on farm machinery, cars. Out on a farm near Orbost.'

It wasn't my father who'd taught me about the inner workings of a motor. My father hadn't taught me much at all. He expected I'd know how to do whatever he wanted me to do, as if my body contained an imprint or the memories of all that he knew because I was his son. He seemed to disregard that it was my mother who grew me and gave birth to me; if there was anyone who'd imprinted their own memories on me, then surely it was her. No, it was not my father. It was an Italian prisoner of war who taught me, showed me. This alien man, with a gentle but deep voice. I waited for him each morning. A local police officer brought him out to our farm from the internment camp at Bete Bolong. He was unlike the other men from my formative years. He turned up to work clean, smooth, tidy. *Giacomo*, he told us his name was. He wore government-issued maroon overalls and a tweed cap. He combed his hair over and trimmed his beard in line with the contours of his face. He hammered fence posts, chipped thistles, fixed machinery. Physical tasks were natural extensions of his body.

I shadowed Giacomo (not only to please my father but also to get away from my father), especially when he worked, with spanners and screwdrivers, on the perfect calibration of each metal part held in the guts of a tractor. Sometimes, he unbuttoned his shirt — once, he took it off altogether and I wanted to touch the dark hairs on his olive skin. Giacomo's skin matched his eyes. He fingered between the motor's parts, never injuring himself. Though we didn't share a spoken language, we each understood the other through our body language. *Piacere* transformed into *ciao*. And *Signor Christoforo* morphed into *passerotto*. I had no idea what these meant except that they were meant for me only. When Giacomo got out of the back seat of Copper's car, he'd shout, *Ciao, passerotto*. With his hand between my shoulders, he would take us away for a day of work. Da would slip inside with Copper, leaving Giacomo to fill the space that he had been draining by his drinking of bitter ale. I supposed that Giacomo provided me with what Ma's death had taken away: someone to show me the way the world worked.

The mechanic put his pen into his overalls' chest pocket. He said his name was Nash and he offered me a cigarette. We stood away from the grease and diesel, smoking and saying nothing of immediate value. There was little talk in the way of actual mechanics, focusing instead on footy: who I followed, who he followed, would I be going to a game. After a short lull, he turned and offered me work: 'Could use an extra set of hands, though if yer cut a finger from either of us, you'll be out on the street.'

After a day's work in the dim garage, where I'd remained quiet, I liked how, when I stepped through the roller door and out onto the street, the sun exploded over my skin. I'd been quiet because I did not know what to say. When Nash and the other lads made crude jokes about the rear end of a car, I'd remain quiet because I didn't know what to do. I wasn't one of those masculine bodies, sweating and hard. Tough, rough. They held a quivering energy, always restless, sometimes flaring out in yells and hoots. I stood somewhat near the edge of the group, and when Nash and his lads scruffed each other in a schoolboy way, they did not scruff me.

I didn't want to head home straightaway. I needed clean, neutral space to clear my mind. So, I walked down through the Botanic Gardens. I sat on park benches, watched swans drift on the surface of the lake. The smell of soil and mulch enveloped me and I forgot, while I sat there, that I was in the middle of a city. From the Gardens I walked beside the river and into suburban streets. In walking around Melbourne, I soon learnt that to not look like a real country fella I had to move, move and not loiter. Sometimes I couldn't help standing still: inside Flinders Street Station, staring up at the departures board, all the trains going in every direction. I could go anywhere. I did not. I stuck to my daily routine — waking, dressing, breakfasting, walking to the mechanic's garage, working, then returning home for tea.

During the first few months, I hadn't the courage to venture much further than what I knew; living in the country, though I'd been keen to escape it, had made me insulated and habitual. I was like the days shortening as winter approached. When I wasn't minding what dripped onto the clean garage floor or trying to make my voice louder so Nash's lads would pay attention to me, I attended technical college one day a week. Lectures presented a physical language describing what was happening, and what was *not* happening, to a motor vehicle. I didn't grasp it at first. I sensed the potential.

The city had so much potential.

*

As the days grew colder and the black grease on my hands stiffened because of the temperature, I began to look forward to going home each day from the garage; I day-dreamed about warm soapy water running over my palms. Dissolved Epsom salts. Because it was in the bathroom that I came to feel most safe. Behind the locked door. Alone. Unseen. Not like out there — in the garage or the wider world. Out there, it was as if I moved through a space that was not intended for me. Buildings and gardens and streets built by men unlike me. Built and governed by men like Nash and his lads, like Da and Kings. If only I had more money, more than I was saving week to week. Savings. What for? I could blow it all on nice clothes, lots of booze, a speeding car. But I wouldn't. I'd continue saving. Building my fortune to move into a house of my own. Rent or buy, I didn't mind. A house that stood on its own. Tall trees and busy shrubs on every side. A modest home, but a home to call my own. Where I'd be my own; with my own. And so: wake, get up, wash, garage, grease, check voice, check body, gears, go home, eat, wash, sleep.

One Saturday morning Kings and I were doing our washing. The small room at the back where Kings had set up a washing copper was insulated and warm. Kings tested the water in the copper with his own fingers. He had only a singlet and cotton boxers on. I was dressed similarly.

Rain against the tin roof of the laundry lean-to, on the glass pane of the tiny window, and in between the bricks of the path outside the door. Clouds had been threatening all week, lingering then stretching over-head, and finally breaking open. The streets and streets and streets of buildings meant I hadn't seen the clouds encroach; I'd just known that this was how they must have arrived, based on my memory of watching storms roll in over the flat lands down at Marlo.

My sister, Iris, always did the washing back at home. I felt her red-hot fingers enlace round my throat: I'd not spoken with her since I'd moved in with Kings. I told him that Iris, after she'd done our family's laundry, used to warm my hands in winter between her hands. Her skin would be raw, hurting her, from the washing.

Kings laughed. 'Did you think that as soon as you moved out of home you'd fall in with a bonny lass who'd pick up your undies and throw them in the copper with-out any questions?'

I shrugged off the accusation. 'Don't need a bonny lass,' I said. 'I got you.'

'You'll need extra boiling on those overalls,' he said. He put in his white business shirts with a pair of wooden tongs, pushed the shirts down into the milky soap-water. Vapour rose up in his face.

I prepared my own clothes. Laid out the overalls, which smelled of the men I worked beside: cigarette smoke and laughter and oil on hands and grease under fingernails. 'I dunno if even a triple boiling will get some of these out,' I said. 'Maybe I'll just wear the one pair till they're hard with grime, then throw them away and get a new pair.'

'Such an effort,' Kings said, 'just to keep up appearances.'

'Only thing I'm keeping up any kind of appearance for is the inside of an engine.'

'You've been here a little while now and you're trying to tell me you've not got a missus?' He took out one of his shirts and held it over a sink behind him. The window above the sink let a grey light in, which landed dully on the whitened material. He ran cold water, wrung it fresh through the shirt. 'I bet some miss comes by every now and then that even you would wipe your greasy mitts for.' He removed the rest of his shirts from the copper, rinsing each in the sink.

I dropped my overalls into the copper; the blue material darkened, soaking up the liquid. So deep was the colour change that I lost sight of the stains. I said, 'Only miss I know is my sister.' I pushed down the blob of overalls with the wooden tongs, hid the material below. Ashamed. Air gulped out from where it could, broke in bubbles at the surface. Drops landed on my forearm; the liquid seared.

'She seeing a bloke?'

'I think she's seeing some farmhand from Orbost.'

He passed one of his shirts through a mangle. A strained, moist noise. 'The bird I'm seeing is a bit older than me.' His voice, because of the work he did at the mangle, was almost as squashed as the shirt he wrung.

'Oh,' I said, 'good for you.'

'Her name's Dotty. A clerk of courts that I kept running into.'

I moved away from the copper to let the overalls boil for a bit. I leant against the wall, which was damp with steam. Damp on my shoulder blades, my arse. I watched Kings's upper arms flex as he turned the handle of the mangle. He bit his top lip. Loose hair flopped down over his forehead. His cotton boxers stuck to his thighs. When he was done with the first shirt, he wrestled it from the rollers and gave it three sharp shakes. He dropped it into a straw basket sitting on the floor.

'So, what's she like?'

Kings, red-faced and squinty-eyed, looked up as if he'd just realised I was still in the room. 'Oh.' He placed his second shirt at the edge of the mangle and started to rotate the handle. 'Some'd say Dot's damaged goods.'

'What d'you mean?'

He grunted. 'She's been married before. Her first husband ran off with a bloke.'

I shifted my weight from one foot to the other. Condensed water had collected in a puddle on the floor beside my foot, and when I stepped in this small pool, my foot slipped forward. I regained my balance. Arms crossed over my chest. 'Bloke?'

Kings pulled the second shirt through the mangle.

'Yeah, mate. He was a poof.'

The material snapped loud when he shook it.

Kings brought much of his work home. He followed what he called 'moral crimes' — drunkenness, prostitution, gross indecency. He didn't strike me as religious, but I never initiated such a conversation because I had a gut feeling he wouldn't like my position on the matter. He was very matter-of-fact. After a long day at the courtrooms, he preferred to bring his notes home, draft up a story, and call it in to the copy boys before the *Bulletin* went to press. His voice carried down the hallway. I lay in my bed, listening to his commands: so precise — each word enunciated, each piece of punctuation declared. His message would not be missed. He even had the copy boys recite his sentences back to him and he corrected any errors. *Caught in the Royal Botanic Gardens. Discovered at a private residence. Revealed in the City Baths. Found in a compromising position by the head gardener. Turned in by an anonymous witness. Arrested by police. Charged with committing an act of gross indecency with each other. Sentenced to one month's imprisonment with hard labour.* His low voice, moving through the house, became a voice inside my head.

*

Nash hadn't let me so much as near a car except to wash it down before someone came to pick it up. Said I was careless and when not careless I was aloof. Said if I was not careful I'd mis-jack a car and be squashed while I was under it. I cleaned, washed, sourced missing parts. It reminded me of being on the farm at Da's: though I'd never realised it at the time, with hindsight, that man had always kept me at menial tasks. Chipping thistles, fixing fallen fences. Had it not been for Giacomo, perhaps I'd still be doing those tasks and living in the same house as Da.

One morning I was sweeping while Nash and the lads smoked out back. A glimmering widgie brought in a small car. She wore her hair cut short, dyed red, a satin shirt and a tight-fitting pair of jeans. She said her boyfriend was the last person to drive and since then the car hadn't been the same.

'It'll have to wait,' I told her, 'the head mechanic's out at smoko.'

She winced. 'Oh no.' She pushed her hair away from her face and looked into her handbag. 'I'll pay you extra.' She showed me a decent roll of cash. 'I need my car.'

I twisted my hands around the broom handle. She seemed worried; around her eyes darker than the rest of her skin. 'Look.' I leant the broom up against the wall. 'What's it doing?'

'Seems to be slipping.'

'The car?'

'Mmhm. I dunno. Maybe the gears?'

I said to her, 'Even if there was a senior mechanic available now, your boyfriend's car—'

'My car,' she corrected. 'I own this car.'

'Your car — it might be out of action for a few hours. Depending on what's wrong.'

'No,' she whipped back. 'I need it as soon as possible.' Those eyes, searching. She wanted something from me; I wasn't sure I could give it to her.

'Miss, you don't understand.'

She pointed at me. 'Why — aren't you a mechanic?'

I nodded.

'You can do it, yes?'

I shook my head. 'I'm not—'

She flashed the roll of money again. I thought about what I could do with it: bond on a place, a trip overseas, a car of my very own, booze to fuel my boredom.

'I'll tip you well,' she said.

I took out a cloth to wipe my hands. Checked over my shoulder to see if Nash or any one of his lads was there, waiting for me to fuck it up. 'We can't have you indisposed for too long,' I said and moved towards the car. She stepped out of my way, thanked me. I used a lift to raise the car off the ground. Began. Once I'd dismantled what I needed, I scanned the flywheel rim, checked each of its teeth. 'Here.' I placed my finger on the thick layer of greasy dust.

'You fixed it?'

Her voice frightened me. I jerked back and hit my head on the underside of the car. 'Fuck,' I whispered. Then said, louder, 'Most of the work is cleaning.' I was speaking more to metal than to her; the sound vibrated around me, but I kept my head under the engine.

'Chris'fer,' Nash yelled from somewhere on the other side.

Prove yourself. I called back, 'Yeah, mate?'

'He's fixing my car,' the woman said. Her voice, in reply, sounded like a wink. 'The nice man under there's taking very good care of me.'

'The nice man shouldn't be under there.'

She cooed, 'Please don't be mad at him.'

'Look, missus—'

'No, really,' she interrupted. 'I *made* him.' She needed this car for something very important. Maybe as she was speaking, she held onto Nash's arm. Pleasing him.

'He—'

'No, no. He didn't do anything but help me out,' she said. 'Like a good man should, no?'

'But—'

'Would you rather he made me wait? I might have had to take my business elsewhere.'

Their conversation didn't bother me; I was almost done. I cleaned the parts I needed to and tightened what I could. When I was finished, the woman paid and kissed my cheek. I shivered. As I watched her drive away, waving high out the window, Nash's hand landed on my shoulder.

He was beside me when he said, 'Yer dripped some grease on the garage floor.'

'The car didn't fall,' I said.

'Shame.' He turned back into the garage. 'Did y'least get her number?'

'Said she's got a boyfriend.'

'What she says an' what she does — two different things, mate.'

I forced an agreeable laugh.

'Yer didn't even notice. Too busy proving something to me.' He sat across from me on a high stool, which was beside a workbench. Lifted up a copy of that day's *Bulletin* and flicked out its pages. 'Least now with the tip money she left yer can shout the lads a round of cold ones up at the Farmer's Arms.'

Surrounded on all sides by tall trees, Kings, Dotty, and I sat in the middle of a low-cut lawn and sucked in the air and the Gardens. We were there for a picnic, organised by Dotty. Sticky green foliage and silky petals. Dotty had chosen a spot beside a man-made pond; long reeds, waterlilies yet to bloom, and two black swans populated the water. I was in a strange mood, which made me believe the pond would soon evaporate. Reeds would soon seed themselves. Swans would soon decay. Waterlilies would forever go un-flowered. We'd arrived early and were waiting for the rest of the picnickers to arrive. Dotty asked if we wanted a glass of bubbly.

'We're not allowed,' said Kings.

A few other groups scattered, as if confetti, on the lawn. Most had children. One group, across the lake, played cricket. Every now and then a pop, not too dissimilar to that of a cork being pulled from a champagne bottle, echoed. Dotty used that game of cricket, the noise each time the batter struck the ball, as cover. *Pop*. We *cheers*-ed and sipped.

Through the scrub, down a path, a woman in a yellow dress swished over to us. A huge fur slung over her shoulders to keep off the autumnal chill. The animal's misshapen head, biting its own tail, rested on the woman's chest. She dropped something, stumbling when she bent to pick it up.

'Millie,' Dotty giggled. She stood up. She had runs along the backs of her woollen stockings. She tiptoed towards her friend. When she reached Millie, the women linked arms and walked in step back to us. Dotty said, as they sat down on the rug, 'This is Millie. Millie,' she said, rubbing her friend's arm, 'this is Christopher.'

Kings handed Millie a glass of bubbly.

I took a deep mouthful from my own glass. A swan, at the lake's edge, honked in our direction.

It was mid-arvo and still the other people (all friends of Kings and/or Dotty) had not come. Millie put on a pair of leather gloves, the cuffs dressed with fur similar to that of the animal round her shoulders. We'd gone over the usual polite conversation: what we do, what we don't do, music, theatre, weather. Our words conducted by Dotty. My stomach growled as the others arrived. I was pleased for the distraction. After brief introductions, we sat back down and Millie came close beside me. Her warmth beside me. Could hear her breath. She went to place her fingers on my forearm as part of her natural conversation, but pulled them away as if recalling we'd just met. I shifted from sitting on my backside to holding up my knees with my hands, ankles crossed. Schoolboy-esque.

'Would you like a plate of lunch?' she said.

I nodded.

'Do you not eat anything?' she said.

I'd never before been asked this. 'Anything is okay.' I didn't know if there was anything I would not eat.

She stood, patted down her dress, and went to where Dotty had laid out the containers of salads and meats. Millie came back with two small plates. I let go of my knees so I was sitting cross-legged and took one of the plates from her. Nodded a thank-you. She sat as if side-saddle, her legs folded underneath her. With a fork, she separated a cube of potato from the small pile of salad. This division allowed her to speak.

'I was nervous of coming today,' she said. 'I don't know many of these people.'

I had a mouthful of mush, so I hummed in reply.

'But I did,' she said.

'Why?'

She lifted her chin. 'Because I was asked.' She managed a broad leaf of lettuce between her lips. As she chewed it, she asked why I came when I did not want to.

'Because I was told.' I cut a potato in half with my fork.

We ate. We both drank the champagne. I asked if she was enjoying the meal. She nodded and asked if I wanted some more.

'I made the potato salad,' she said.

I told her I didn't need any more. She took my plate, stacked it on top of hers, smiled. When she came back, she did not sit. She held out her hand for me and suggested we go for a walk.

'I'm stuffed.' I patted my belly.

She giggled. 'Better walking that off than being around people and feeling yourself beached.'

Either way, I didn't want to go, and I decided she was wrong. Being alone with one person can be more awful than being with a group of unknown people. But I got up with her because some of the other picnickers had seen her offering; I could not refuse when it was what they all expected of us.

Up a path, over a hill, behind the flora. Concealed. We didn't speak while walking, though I felt her step closer to me, as if she wanted to move her body in time with mine. Down the hill we met the far side of the lake. Our party of people were across from us: the last group of people in the Gardens. By now the champagne was warming us so we didn't notice the cooling afternoon. Small stones beside the lake were so well-cut that I had the impression they'd been hand carved and placed in a perfect composition. I bent down and extracted one from the scene.

'What are you doing?' she said.

'Do you know how to skip stones?'

She shook her head. 'Dad,' she said, 'always said it was unladylike.'

I winked at her. 'Is your father here to see?'

She giggled. 'Show me.'

I took her hand in mine, warm, placed the stone between her thumb and index fingers, hard. 'Hold the rock in a C-shape.' I picked up a rock of my own and assumed the same position. 'Throw it sideways,' I told her.

She did so, but her rock thumped, sunk.

'Flick your wrist.' Without releasing my stone, I showed her what I meant. 'Just as you let go.' This time I did let go, and my stone kicked up on the water and skipped three times. When I turned back to her, she had both her hands raised to her mouth.

She looked away, turned away. Despite her efforts, she laughed; high notes scattered across the lake further than I could ever imagine skipping a stone. Sparrow's laugh. And as she laughed and tried to apologise, I stood on the stony bank and held my throwing wrist in my other hand.

'Why are you laughing?' I asked.

'I'm so sorry,' she said, 'it just looks so queer when you do that.' She mimicked how I'd flicked my wrist.

I pressed my fingers into my wrist, conscious of how its structure was involved in the movement of my hand.

In silence, we returned to the picnic. Others were drinking booze. Kings handed me the bottle he'd been drinking from. Warm glass against my lips, slippery because of his saliva on the rim. I swigged deep, and swallowed. He went to take the bottle back, but I sipped once more from the mouthpiece before handing it over to him. He wiped where I'd drank from before offering the bottle to Dotty.

Dotty skolled from the bottle and then dropped it in the grass. 'Races!' she screeched.

No one seemed that interested.

'You and me, Dot,' I said. I stood up, eager to get away from Millie, who, with the alcohol, had seemed to become warmer.

Dotty batted away my words and yelled, 'Millie. Millie and you. Millie and Chris'fer.'

Millie hiccupped. She did not look at me, only at Dotty, as she said, 'I'm not wearing proper dress.'

I brushed my backside and went to re-sit, but Kings slapped one of my calves and told me he would race.

'You were never good at footy, Chris, so you'll be an easy beat.' He took off his leather shoes and his tweed jacket and merino scarf, and rolled up his sleeves to his elbows. He wore suspenders to hold up his pants.

He had his back to me, so I snapped one of the suspender straps. Said, 'Were you born in 1880?'

His broad hand, flattened out, swung round and hit the side of my ribs. I coughed from its force. In front of us, Dotty held up a white handkerchief. She told us that to start the race she'd release the hanky, but we were not allowed to run until it landed on the ground. She raised the white hanky higher. Kings shook out his arms, his legs, his head, as if a top-performing athlete. I put my hands on my hips. We took our positions. His lower, both fists planted on the ground, one knee bent. I put one leg back and bent the other, hands by my sides.

Dotty let go of the hanky. A pink light from the setting sun caught in the floating material.

Kings's body jerked. Mine laughed. The hanky danced, touched down on the grass. I missed the start while he bolted, grass flecks flicking up from his feet. My own heavy feet wished I'd taken off my shoes. We headed for a lap of the lake. His white shirt, stretched across his shoulders, shifted from one side to the other with the motion of his running body. Rhythmically, I moved my feet in time to the cutting movement of his shoulder blades. Tight pants creased. Further round the body of water, further away from our picnicking group, our heavier breath and gentle grunts each time our feet hit the ground became louder, until it was all I could hear. Together. I captured a pace; his slowed. I made ground. Was close to him, beside him. Forearms rubbing. I checked his face: eyes narrow, set on the corner we were about to turn. Judging the distance, speed. My foot clipped something (the ground, a rock?) and propelled me forward, upsetting my balance. I tumbled and felt Kings's own feet plunge into my belly, winding me. I rolled across the grass. He rolled on top of me. When my momentum stopped, I was flat on my back, looking up into the sky. Puffed. Kings's face, shadowy, hovered over mine. Our noses touched.

'Now don't play dirty, Chrissy.' He flung a handful of grass into my face and ran off.

I rolled onto my stomach, propped my torso up on my elbows, and watched him sprint the edge of the lake.

On our walk home, I spotted a pub on the street corner. I checked my watch: only twenty to six. Still serving. I told Kings I was going to pop into the pub for a quick one. 'You coming?'

He looked at Dotty; she shook her head. He said to me, 'Nah, mate. You enjoy.'

Inside, red material hanging over the windows darkened the bar. There were a few lights hanging over the bar benches, a dead light, which scarcely reached the billiards table in the centre of the room. I pulled out a bar stool and told the publican, 'One draught, please.'

The bar door opened. A tall, dark man came in. A tailored suit, wrapping his handsome body. I looked at the publican, who wiped a glass as he stared at the newcomer.

'Tap's off,' the publican said.

The man replied, 'It's quarter to six, mate.'

'Like I said, tap is off.' The publican placed the shiny glass on a shelf.

'Can I get *anything*?'

'Best I can,' he said, looking the man up and down, 'is port.'

The man scoffed, 'C'mon.'

'Port or none.' The publican shrugged.

The man paused for a moment. He took out his coin from a drawstring bag and sat it down in a neat pile on the wooden bar.

The publican took the money, tilled it. He poured a small measure — a half-measure from what I could tell. The customer gave an incredulous smile. The publican replaced the port's cork and then the bottle on a high shelf behind him.

The man picked up the glass, which was tiny and might have broken under his masculine fingers. 'Cheers, boys,' he said. Raised his glass at the publican, turned and raised his glass to me, then winked.

I dropped my gaze, only lifted it when I heard his glass re-touch the wooden bar. The man gave a short nod to the publican. As he turned, he gave me another wink. The door swung shut behind him.

His wink was a lure trawling deep water.

*

I followed the man to the Gardens. It was dim, dark, and I lost sight of him near a pavilion built atop a mounded hill. It had a tiered garden, winding paths, hidden alcoves. Two wide front windows peered over the canopies, issuing golden light. From the bottom of the garden, a gravel path led up through the shrubs and trees towards the entry. Australian natives populated the tiered garden: scraggy tea-tree and hakea and pigface growing wild in the breath of the near-distant sea.

I neared halfway up the path. Strewn amid the native plants were geranium and diosma. Slim twigs heavy with gum leaves hung over. Closer to the entry, music, muffled by the walls, flickered in and out. On the veranda, a door slammed, and the suddenness of it stopped me. Could have been a gunshot. But then came a male voice, calling out. Feet stamped. There was another person with him — both faces the colour of the ocean at dusk: swaying, deep, uncertain. I squatted down on the path's edge, peeping up at them through the mixed-up branches of hakea. Someone yelled again, then walked out of sight around the other side.

Something moved behind me. Before I was able to work out what it was, a human body, firm, tumbled over the top of me. The body said *sorry* before either of us had even thought of who was at fault. I sat up, checked my suit for the extent of stains. None. But when I looked over at the body — a man — who was sitting in the opposite garden bed, I couldn't say the same for him.

He had mud on his knees and lapel. He said he was sorry. Rubbed at the mud on the fabric and said, 'It was my fault — I was running.' He focused, chin tucked, eyes on the mud staining his lapel, and I focused likewise on him. He was visible in the shadowy undergrowth. I took in his well-manicured flop of curly brown hair, shorn closer to his head at the back and near his ears. His fringe was pushed to one side. His abrupt appearance, his hasty apology: these were not what startled me. I picked him, instinctively, as *that way*. My way. I watched, waiting for him to reveal more of himself to me. A likeness. Perhaps in his dress. Perhaps in his manners. Perhaps a combination of both. I recoiled, as if catching sight of my own reflection.

'Were you just in the pub?' I demanded.

He flicked his hand out. 'Trying to get one in before the wedding,' he said as he pointed up at the pavilion.

'Strange time for a wedding,' I said.

'More money than sense,' he replied.

I nodded away from him, back to him, away. This man was a connection in an otherwise alien landscape. Perhaps why he'd winked at me. Garden-bed moisture seeped through to my underwear. I assumed, 'Are you helping out here tonight?'

He shook his head. Touched the mud on his clothes. Quite short, he replied, 'I'm a relation of the bride.'

I nodded, disbelieving.

'You?'

I lied, 'Friend of a friend.'

His nail scraped on his lapel where some mud had stained. I rubbed my fingers together, feeling for the thick slime of any mechanic's grease that I might have missed washing from my hands.

'You can't go in like that,' I told him. Got to my feet. Held out my hand to help him stand.

He stood taller than me. 'Thanks,' he said.

'The bogs down there,' I said, 'has paper towel and water. We can clean up those stains.'

He seemed to find my suggestion amusing. Said, 'Lead the way.'

As I did, I noticed how his figure brooded over me from behind, like a shadow or a silhouette, accentuated by the dark night and the gradient as we descended.

He swirled his body through the entry to the bogs: at one stage, his back was to me and then, pivoting his feet, he faced me before turning once more and slipping inside. It was seductive and elaborate; I felt the air his body had displaced brush against my exposed skin. I followed. In there, I found him half-sitting on the basin bench, legs stretched out so his suit pants rose to reveal socks of emerald green. His frame, which my palms tingled for, partially obstructed the mirror. As I began to wet a bunch of paper tower, he turned his face to the side of my head and his lips nearly touched my earlobe.

My breath came faster. I squeezed water from the paper towel and turned to him. If he leant in, his lips would have touched mine. I felt his eyes on me, questioning me. I showed him the towel I'd wet and then pressed it to his lapel, wiping at the mud stain.

'It's coming out,' I said.

His shoulders dropped. He exhaled, and I could smell on his breath the sweet port I'd watched him drink.

'Here,' he said. His warm fingers touched the back of my hand and took it away from where I was cleaning. He removed the towel from my hand. He turned to face the mirror and began wiping the stain out for himself. He cursed under his breath, rubbed harder so that parts of the paper towel began to break off and stick in the threads of his jacket. 'Damn,' he said and tossed the paper towel to the ground. 'It's *not* coming out.'

'S'pose you can't go to the wedding,' I said, 'with a dirt stain on you, I mean.'

He smiled at me. 'Shame the pub's not open.'

'We could've had another port. Together.'

He laughed. And I wondered if, in that moment, we both realised that neither of us had come to the Gardens for the wedding.

As he and I walked away from the Gardens, towards the train station, I wondered what might have happened if we had gone into the wedding. Perhaps he would have offered to get us both a drink. We would have stood amid the eyes, closer to the back, and drank, and talked, and drank, and talked. I would have slurred my words, too much for them to make much sense, out of fear that what I was saying bored him. And because the other partyers might have been seeing the world through blurrier eyes, too, he might have slipped his arm round my waist — just as Kings did sometimes to an intoxicated Dotty. I would have allowed my head to dip to rest on his chest — just as Dotty did upon Kings. Or none of this might have happened. Or only some of it. Or more. If only, as you were rubbing the mud from his lapel, you had said what you wanted to say: *I never expected to meet someone who has this kind of effect on me.* The feeling reminded me of how, after Ma died, Iris would take cousin Jimmy and me down to the beach at Marlo on hot weekends. In my underwear, I'd stand waist-deep waiting for the swell to crash against my body. Water weight pushed me over and rushed all round me, drowned the throbbing heaviness within me, if only for a few moments.

In the train carriage, we sat across from each other. Seeing him before me again, I felt my confidence grow, strengthened by the memory of his hand on mine. I had always been aware of men — ever since Kings had shown me the hair growing around his things. I did not yet know who this man would become to me, though. Or even if he *would* become.

We introduced ourselves. We met each other's gaze

for a number of blank seconds: I was certain my eyes revealed too much; his were settled and assured. So, 'Morgan,' I said. 'Sorry about the mud on your clothing.'

He yawned, covered his mouth with the back of his hand. He was not quite done yawning, but he waved his hand as if to absolve me: *don't worry*.

I faltered.

From his jacket pocket, he took out a rolled cigarette. He placed it between his lips and then brought out a box of matches, again from his pocket. He ignited the cigarette and drew back. As the plume settled, he took the cigarette away from his lips, turned it, and handed it to me.

I inhaled what he had inhaled. I blew out a lungful of smoke. When I made a move to hand the cigarette back, he declined and took out another for himself. I placed mine back between my lips. I asked if he'd travelled far for the wedding.

He held another match near his face. 'I'm from New South. Deniliquin?' he asked as if sure I would know it. 'Moved to Melbourne when I was a little boy. The bride's family is close to mine. I suppose.'

'Your family still in New South?'

He shook his head. 'My family's all over,' he said with a steady gaze. 'I moved down here with my father. Only us two.'

'You live with him now?'

He nodded. 'And you?'

'Alone.'

'No family?'

'I'm alone in the city.'

'Where is your family?'

'My sister — she's in Marlo. Gippsland.'

'What about your parents?'

I told him my mother died when I was young and that my father was away.

'Away?'

I didn't give him an answer. 'I didn't want to be in Marlo forever,' I told him. 'Couldn't wait to leave.'

'There's always something to get away from.'

I nodded, but thought it best to change the subject; I might have had to reveal more than I wanted to. I asked if he liked Melbourne.

His head wobbled. 'Bits,' he said. 'Others not so much — Melbourne doesn't feel like home.'

As he spoke, I noted his gestures — the way his hands moved, the way he nodded — which were as if he felt the physicality of each word he spoke. I noticed that when he finished one idea and started the next, his fingers tapped on top of each of his syllables, testing their structure.

He explained that he worked in real estate. 'People become so possessive about such material things,' he said.

I tried to picture him selling me a house. I tried to picture him selling Kings and Dotty a house. I wondered how'd they react to a coloured man.

'Do you sell them?' I asked.

'My father leases them out. I'm his maintenance man. Faulty gas heaters, leaky taps, broken tiles.' Morgan smoked. 'I'm there when the tenants aren't.'

His hands in an empty house, his hands combing through possessions, his hands raising possessions from where they lay, his hands laying those possessions back, patting them flat, and pushing the drawer closed.

He said, 'What do you do?'

'Mechanic.'

He seemed puzzled. 'You don't look it.'

I laughed. 'I learnt young,' I told him, 'from an Italian prisoner of war. It's the only thing I'm okay at.'

'Learning from a prisoner or being a mechanic?' Morgan sat with a half-burnt rollie between his lips. He straightened his jacket with both hands.

I caught my reflection in the glass. 'I've never considered it,' I said. 'I s'pose both.' I smiled, tight-lipped. 'But the noise in the city. It unsettles me. Sometimes I look at the roads, the endless stretch of the suburbs, and—'

'Want to tear it all up?'

Having a strong sense that I'd indeed said too much — or not enough — I let my eyes roll into my lap. I said, 'Being unable to see the horizon is unnatural.'

Morgan sighed. His eyes dropped to his own entwined hands. 'I'm tired,' he said. Shook his head. 'Look, I shouldn't be here.'

I choked. 'Why?'

'I could get you into trouble.'

'How?'

'By being. Here.'

I rubbed the pad of one finger over the nail of another. 'The next stop is mine,' I said. 'You should get off there with me.'

'You're so sure of quite a lot.' He extinguished his cigarette under his foot. The train bumped us, now silent, from our postures. Electric carriage light wobbled over our bodies and cast our shadows together, apart.

The train rattled in. The carriage doors opened and a mild pollution puffed at us. The platform, its occupants' belligerent grey stares, awaited. The carriage could have gone on rocking, forever soothing the nerves inside me, but already Morgan was standing as he gathered himself. Not a word passed between us as we attended to our belongings, clearing any sign that we were there.

'Christopher.'

My name was spoken faintly: it could have been a voice inside my own head. The intimacy made me turn to Morgan, who'd spoken it. His head twitched around the compartment, as if trying to find something. To compensate for not producing it — whatever it was — or perhaps to cut me off before I could jump in, he held out his hand. He had a calm directness when he said, 'It's been swish.'

I had to hold back a smile. *Swish*. I shook Morgan's hand and when I did, I felt something other than skin touch between my palm and his. It was a thin piece of paper; soft torn edges could have been as sharp as blades. When he moved his hand back, his fingertips pressed the small piece of paper into my hand so that it didn't fall away. I hid the paper in my pocket.

I went home. Washed. When I came to putting away my suit jacket, I recalled the stains Morgan had on him after he'd tripped over me. Mud had streaked the stitching at his shoulder and his knees. Mud that marked him. In a strange way, it had confirmed for me what I suspected was in his heart, his body. It was the same thing that was in my heart. It was the same thing that sat there in our hearts' chambers and organs and veins and bones — like scum in the grout that not even the harshest wire could remove. Though my suit remained clean, I ran the tip of my index finger over the places where Morgan's suit would contain the scent of earth, of hakea, of smoke. From the pocket, I retrieved the piece of paper, upon which he'd written his phone number and address.

Kings sometimes reported to me of men being captured at the public toilets by the Vice Squad. He might have had a smirk when he said, 'Vice entrap these guys, y'know? They pretend to be poofs — Vice, I mean — and then arrest the actual poofs who go to the bogs to fuck.'

He emphasised these two words: *poof* and *fuck*. 'Down at the courthouse,' he'd continued, 'they say poofs crawl all over the gardens at night.' Then he'd read aloud the title of his most recent *Bulletin* article: '"Growing menace of sex perverts". How's that for a headline?'

Past midnight, I re-entered the Gardens via a loose side gate. I'd returned because I had a sense that I'd missed something, that there was another possible outcome to the evening. I stumbled paths between miniature valleys. Iron leaves coated by moonlight. I stood away from the public toilet — the bogs. Waited. After some time, two men walked towards each other. Under the bright moon their lips moved. From them I learnt a simple way. Communicate with your eyes. Contact. And then, sauntering along, say, *How y'goin', mate?* Casual. Combined, this was enough to land a customer. After that, everything was pretty straightforward: you do it, you finish, you do not speak, you go your own — separate — way. When those two men had gone, I loitered close to where they had stood. Leaning against the bogs' wall, I shivered from the cold. Needed a piss. I slipped into the building. A limp light lurked inside. I pissed in a cubicle loo. When I came out, there was another person, a slender thing, who stood at the mirror. Part man, part woman, this person wore make-up, a long-haired wig, but the clothes were masculine. Leather and denim-patched.

I asked, 'What's, ah, what's going on in here?'

The person tapped an index finger on a set of

rounded lips. 'You're not meant to ask, hun.' Face reflected in the shadowy mirror. 'But because you're handsome, I'm Jacqui. Q, U, I.' The long figure turned. 'I can *always* make an exception for a Rock Hudson type.' Jacqui laughed almost silently. And said, 'Not in the way you're thinking, though.'

'I don't—'

'Hun.' Jacqui floated over to me, before leading me outside.

'Who are you?'

'Questions, questions,' Jacqui said. 'I move here and there.' Jacqui flicked out a lighter and ignited the end of a cigarette, which sat between those reddened lips. 'You?'

'I'm a mechanic.'

'You fix broken things?'

'Only cars.'

Jacqui dragged on the cigarette; closed eyes suggested equilibrium, while a lengthy exhale of white smoke conveyed pure relief. 'Of course.' Jacqui dropped the cigarette on the ground and moved to a nearby garden bed.

I stood idle on an open lawn, perhaps near to where Kings and Dotty and I had picnicked during the day.

'What are you doing out in the open?' Jacqui said.

I didn't want to go into the darkness.

'You'll get stung by Vice.'

It was too much to explain my reasons, so I said, 'It'd be a thrill.'

'There's nothing thrilling about a prison cell. No. Come up under here.'

If something happened to me — a punch to the face or kick to the guts — how long would it be before someone found me? How would they find me? No one knew I was there. I could die up here or be deemed a suicide. I could run back down the hill. Slip back out the gate. The grass was soft and would hide the sound of my feet. But there was something about Jacqui, about the trust that I was following, still, that was compelling: each of us wanted something from the other. Sweat patched under my arms. A breeze trickled around us; I adjusted my shirt's collar. I glanced the short way down the hill to scout for people — although part of me wanted to be as brash as Kings was with Dotty — but I saw only the lake. Moonlight slithered on its surface.

Jacqui pulled me in by my shirt. We kissed. My first kiss. I moved my body outwards. Jacqui grabbed me round the middle. Muggy breath and then a moist, warm tongue on my neck. A hand rubbed against my waistline, fingers worked around my underwear. Jacqui's erection poked. I pulled further away. The hand pushed inside my underwear, and a rogue palm, rough and arousing, squeezed. I tore myself away.

'What are you doing?' I tugged Jacqui by the collar, from the tree. A nelly voice squawked retaliation. The lake was behind us and I thrust Jacqui towards it. A screech, no words, tumbled down the hill and ended in a shattering splash. I wiped my mouth on my sleeve as I headed back up the track.

Home.

It was still, except for some nocturnal bird's cawing in the trees. I crept across the lawn, realising from the shade of sky that it was closer to morning than it was to midnight. Up on the porch, I found the front door locked. I had no key. I climbed over the side gate, which rattled under my body's weight. I fell down the other side, into the ground. The window to the laundry was ajar. I prised it open enough to squeeze myself through. As I forced my body in, my feet knocked the wooden washing tongs into an empty copper tub. The sound clapped like a pair of cymbals. A light in the house switched on.

Kings called from within, 'Who's there?'

'Me,' I replied. I got to my feet as quick as I could.

Kings came into the doorframe. He had a cricket bat raised out in front, ready to strike me.

'What's the bat for?'

'I thought you were a burglar,' he replied. 'What are you doing?' he whispered.

'I forgot my key.'

Kings checked over his shoulder. He seemed to expect that someone else had followed him. 'Where have you been?' But before I could answer him, he called out into the house, 'It's alright, Dot.' Then, facing me, he said, 'It was just a feral cat.'

'Dotty's still here?' I tried to peer round Kings, but he pressed the end of the bat into my chest.

I said, 'You know I live here, too.'

'Because I still let you,' he said, 'but it doesn't give you the right to sneak round like you're up to no good.'

'I beg yours?'

'Dotty nearly called the police.' He gestured with his bat. 'I nearly hit you for six.'

'That's a tad ridiculous,' I scoffed. 'So what, I got a bit carried away and came home late?'

'Carried away where?'

I did not answer him.

'I think it's time for bed now, Chris.'

My clothes, out-turned sleeves and tangled undies, piled in the corner of the bathroom. I found a nailbrush in the cupboard under the vanity. I checked, once more, that the door was locked. I slid into the bath's steaming water. A wave sloshed over the side. I soaped up the nailbrush and began scrubbing the firm bristles against my neck, my shoulders, my armpits and chest; creamy foam thickened over my skin. I slipped, steadied myself. Naked and locked away. I scrubbed my abdomen until my skin turned red. Scrubbed, scrubbed, scrubbed, and then sunk beneath the water to wash the bubbly foam away.

*

Morgan and I met in the mid-1950s. Around the same time, there was a major criminal trial happening in one of the city's courts. A newly arrived prisoner at Pentridge was awaiting bail after being entrapped by the Vice Squad.

> A former Lance Corporal, Mr Michele
> Alazone, who resides at 2/23 Glentree
> Road, Malvern West, has been alleged in
> court today to have assaulted a 19-year-
> old private from his artillery team during
> a training session at Camp Bonadee six
> months ago. Mr Alazone, a naturalised
> Italian alien, was arrested last Saturday.
> His trial started today. He has in the
> intervening time been demoted from
> his military duties.

Because of the case's high profile, the pillory was not, in this instance, a column but rather front-page news. Kings pored over case notes, notebooks, scraps of foolscap, and clippings. We'd been eating in the front room every night, the radio tuned into the news service, because his notes had overtaken the dining room. He always had a glass of water beside him, despite my offers of wine or beer. He'd rub both hands over his face, sighing like a heifer getting ready to birth.

I asked why there was so much detail in the article. 'Name, address, job.' I pointed out that that level of detail wasn't published for the other crime reports he'd put his by-line on.

He said, 'Precisely.'

I found settling down — being calm or relaxed — difficult given the coincidence of Kings's front-page story and Morgan handing over his personal details. Was that tantamount to a confession? Perhaps we were guilty even prior to writing. But if we *did* write to each other, and over time those letters accumulated, all someone had to do was chance upon them and speculate as to their cause. Perhaps Kings himself would find them, would read them, would say something to the wrong person about my being in possession of such letters, and then all that wrong person had to do was declare the news in the press or to the police. I might not have been a corporal in the army, but that did not seem to matter. What mattered was speculation and editorial policy.

Morgan ran laps in my head. His voice had first attracted my attention, his countenance fixed it, and his manners confirmed him to me. *Swish*: a code word, shorthand. For now, perhaps forever. When Morgan handed me that piece of paper, somebody could have seen. We could have become front-page news.

This weighed on me as I considered writing to Morgan; a letter could become evidence and send us both to prison. Kings's articles sharpened my understanding of the things he was writing about and how I related to those ideas. You could murder someone and remain anonymous until your conviction, but you could not take a lover if he was the same as you without the whole city knowing the place at which you made love. There were people like me — of course — and as long as I didn't get caught alongside those people I'd remain the plains wanderer, that elusive little bird that exists between myth and reality. At times I'd rage against the words and the ideas with ease and confidence; at other times, the words, the ink — the heavy ink — coated my tongue, clouded my eyes like cataracts. Often, vileness was all I could see and taste.

Wash the taste out with a bottle of beer; burn the language with whiskey. Or, after an endless succession of days, days, days, after the repetitive administration of suburban anaesthesia, I'd break into the Gardens. Always mindful, as Ma had said, of getting my shirt caught on a loose fence wire. Among the greenery, sometimes under it, I could forge my rage and confusion into compliance. After the Alazone story, I didn't go down to the bogs for a play. I found a dark gully and stretched out on the ground, watching the stars illume. Being alone in the dark was often enough for me to catch my breath.

Dusk, near the lake. I checked that Jacqui, who I'd pushed into the lake, had not bloated in the water's shallows. Frogs bellowed back at me. Shadows across water. One shadow grew larger in the murk, shifted round the edge towards me. A man's body cast this shadow. When he was closer to me, he plugged his hands into his pocket.

Said, 'Y'right?'

'Swell,' I replied.

He grunted. Kicked the ground with the cap of his boot. 'Lookin'?'

I was reminded of the news reports, of police officers from the Vice Squad posing as men cruising at the beat. Cleanse the city of its dirty pervs. Undercover cops wanted to seduce you — with their big muscles, tight pants, authority. If you chose to go off with them, they'd snap a pair of cuffs on your wrists and shove you into the back of a cop car. Other officers had ulterior motives. Those cops played the embarrassed man, the scared boy, the shy trade. Those cops had brought their mates with them, who were hiding in the bushes with cricket bats and batons. Those cops didn't care if you were arrested or not: they just wanted blood.

I told this man I didn't know what he meant. I'd learnt from Jacqui that you didn't ask questions: to be so brazen was to confess guilt. I stood up. Brushed off my backside. I turned away from him. Said, 'You have a good night, mate.'

Two hands grasped my shoulders from behind, brought me in close. A bristly cheek pressed my neck, warm breath crept down my shirt. One hand, which smelt of mechanic's grease, held my mouth shut. I knew that scent and almost fell into it. He turned me back towards the lake, on which the moon distended. He was going to drown me. He said nothing; the only thing to exit his mouth was his tongue sliding from my cheek to my ear, where it twirled around and then out over my neck. My breath snuffed against the palm of his hand. He propelled me forward and I splashed into the water. When I resurfaced, he had disappeared.

I climbed out of the lake, wiped specks of scum from my face, pulled a long reed off my arm, and headed up the hill to the public loo.

Inside was that squashed nance at the basin. Jacqui wore a floor-length mink coat — its dead fur gave the impression of another monster-like creature, lurking in the beat.

'Someone beat me to it.'

'To what?'

'To trying to drown you.'

'Some messed-up bloke pushed me in the lake.'

'Haven't we all had a messed-up bloke push us into a lake.' Jacqui handed me a bunch of paper towel, did not offer help. 'Narcissus, have you found your mirror?'

I covered my face with the towel. I wanted to escape my current body, escape all the newsprint I'd ever read. Even escape Jacqui, who I was otherwise thankful for.

'About what you did to me.' Jacqui held up a hand, angled a sharp ninety degrees. Said, 'Such creature as I am.' A sweeping hand gesture included me as a creature, too, as if we two people were one. 'I have not in all the sum of my virility any masculine or feminine trait.' Jacqui took hold of my hand and then ran fingertips up my arm. 'In every feature, line, sinew, in every moment and accent and capability, I walk the world's ways as myself.'

Fingertips, fingernails — they lingered at my chin.

I breathed out. The heavy exhalation contained so much: the burning banks of the Snowy River, upon which my mother had perished; the barn swallows sipping at the water; Giacomo's golden chain; hands and guns and cars and ... All of it, in that exhalation, plummeted to the floor.

I leant towards Jacqui, but fell into nothingness.

'Come back to the city with me.'

'Squad'll be out tonight.'

'They're out every night.'

'I'm soaking wet.'

Jacqui peeled off the long mink coat: underneath, a flapper-style dress, equally floor-length, shimmered crystal-black. 'Have this for the walk.'

'Won't you be cold?'

Jacqui began buttoning the coat for me and said, 'It's not yours to keep, hun.'

The door stood beside a frock shop. In the window, three tall mannequins. The get-ups those plastic people wore were, to me, either put together by someone who was born last century or designed to distract any passer-by from the people climbing the rickety stairs to the café above. I was more damp than wet by the time we arrived. After Jacqui had turned to me and asked for the mink coat back, we ascended, as if someone was watching. Halfway up, Jacqui, breathless, warned me not to stare at the patrons. 'There are all sorts — from bodgies and activists to dancers and students.' The room upstairs seated more than fifty people. Most sat on mauve-painted wooden chairs at tables. A blue carpet runner down the middle, laid over the parquet floor. Having never seen something so regal or garish, I kept to its edges, fearful I'd fall if I were to walk down the middle. At the side of the room, spaced along the walls, stood standard lamps with ruffled shades lit by differently coloured globes. At the front of the room was a small stage with a grand piano taking up most of the space. A chorus of people called out when Jacqui entered.

'Oh, there *she* is!'

Jacqui blushed, covered her mouth with a fan she'd pulled out from … somewhere. People turned to blow her kisses; some landed on Jacqui's cheeks. She obliged. I was out of their line of sight; Jacqui didn't introduce me. When we sat down at one of the tables, she ordered a threepence coffee for each of us.

A tall blonde woman took the order and assured us that *any friend is a friend — coffee's on the house.*

As we waited, Jacqui pointed to the table at the back, full of people who'd stood up to kiss her on the cheek. 'All kamp,' she drawled.

'Kamp?'

Turning back to look right into me, she said, 'We're the ones you read about in the papers.'

'How do you know them?'

'Our kind always finds one another; you found me,' she said. 'I usually sit with them. As you're new, you're not allowed.'

Coffee arrived.

I said, 'They called you *she*.'

'You can, too. If you want.'

'That's not—'

But Jacqui held two of her fingers up to my lips. 'It's all part of the package, hun. Of being …' Instead of finishing the sentence, she pointed at herself. A finger flopped away rather than point at me. 'All you have to do is surround yourself with people who tell you the things you want to hear. And, I mean, they don't even have to know that what they're saying is what you want to hear, and you might not even realise that you keep going back to them for that same reason.'

'Pardon?'

'Eventually you have all these people around you that all say the same things. Which means you don't have to think anymore. Take this room.' Jacqui's gaze scanned the floor. Though the light was dim, her voice, when she spoke again, ignited. 'They're all sorts, hun.' She turned back to me. 'People like me. Like you.'

'C'mon.'

'C'mon, hun. You were at the park, after dark — how did you know to go there?'

'I followed a man who winked at me,' I said.

'And his wink told you something about yourself, about the both of you. What is more is that you're here. Now. Has to be the kampest place in Melbourne.'

Women in tailored suits. A singer onstage whose voice was as deep, if not deeper, than mine. Men in ball gowns. Each different. In this café, together, they made a whole. Distinct and complete. They were the same in that they were outcast, outlawed, underground. Kamp. They'd made a world that sat beside the visible world. They revelled in its illegality because what made it illegal was what made them who they were. They perceived it differently. They told themselves different stories. Fell asleep to different music. Laughed at different jokes. And raged, raged against the rest of it. Until the sun rose: faint touch on the windowpanes a gentle reminder of tomorrow. So they wiped their faces of the evidence, cleared the tables of the brews, snuffed the candles and closed the curtains. They threw their sodden tissues — smeared with make-up or filled with semen — into the garbage bin. They placed huge coats over their slim outfits and marched down the rickety stairs, out onto the bluestone pavement. Men on men, men on women, women on women, people on people. I wanted the same freedom as them, but without the publicity. The feather boas and embroidered dresses were for one kind of kamp; closed off doors and quiet, unseen spaces were for another. Were for me. Despite the joy of recognition, I could not get past my own apprehension. An apprehension not for them or for what they were doing; rather, an apprehension for what I could not enjoy with them. I did not want to do what these people wanted me to do; I did not want to act as they did; I did not want to exist as they existed.

'I am *not* kamp.'

I went down the stairs and leant against the frock-shop window out on the street.

Jacqui had come out behind me. Her hand was up as if she meant to place it on my cheek, just as my mother used to. If I rested my head in the curve of her palm, I knew I'd break. Jacqui's eyes were enormous and brown, just like Morgan's. I grabbed her by the shoulders and placed my lips against her soft, rounded, reddened lips.

She broke away. 'Chris!' But her protest was unfounded: the street was silent, semi-dark.

'No one saw,' I told her.

'I don't care about people seeing,' she said.

I sat down, my back against the shopfront; if I looked up, I could see under those dresses. I gazed at the overhanging veranda, where cobwebs wavered. 'Don't hate me,' I said.

'I am at the mercy of my emotions. I'll let you know their verdict once they've heard your argument.'

'I should've come here with someone else.'

'Is that all?' Jacqui laughed. 'I brought you here to show you a world that we've made for our own people. It's in your eyes: a boy. He's in your very being. Whatever your trouble is with him, just know that this place is always here.'

'I don't need a place like this.'

'People like us can't have what all those others have.' Across the street she indicated a man and woman who'd just come into view: the man had his arm round the woman's waist as he kissed the top of her head. Jacqui lit a cigarette. Her fine features were pointed in the shadows the flame cast. She said, in a plume of smoke, 'But *they* can't have this.' She pointed to one of the mannequins in the shopfront. 'We should wear it as loud as this quean in the window.'

I caught a train home. Pulled my collar up against the side of my cheek, rested my elbow on the window's sill, covered my eyes with my hand. A pervasive sadness sat in the middle of my chest like the demon mære visiting in the middle of the night, suffocating me. And like the mære, it came from somewhere else, unexplained. If I looked too closely at it, awoke and tried to stop it, it had already slipped away — as if it knew me better than I knew myself. I didn't want to cry or scream. Just heavy. Just tired. I'd never seen a place like that café or a person such as Jacqui. Another world within this world. I wanted a private freedom, though — a fiefdom closed off, behind doors, quiet and unseen by men who placed their arms round women. I could protect a private space; I could not protect a café. I could not protect the Gardens. I could not protect myself in the outside world from the people who didn't want me to exist in it.

I used to have this dream and in it I was alone, running through an endless field. Above, someone rode with thunderclouds between their legs and shot white bolts of lightning down, down, down. Earth spat up when the bright bolts hit. Electric burnt. One time, I was running away from the lightning bolts; one time, I was throwing down the lightning bolts. Once, throwing them at Kings (or Kings at me?); once at Da (or Da at me?); once I threw them with Giacomo sitting beside me. Laughing. But always asking myself: *what are you doing here?*

In my dream, I'd hide from the aloneness, sensing out darker places where no eyes could land upon me. I did not seek to be conceptualised or understood; I sought the undergrowth of shrubs, like a plains wanderer. Under drooping foliage, I figured someone who bothered looking could save me, could find me, was like me. But in summer when the sky was possibly glass, when I'd rested beneath the hakeas, and their spiny limbs criss-crossed the blue above, it was Ma who came looking. Her feet, tiny feet, would get louder as she drew closer. Her footfalls were my rescuers, and I was the damsel in distress, dreaming of the journey that Ma, in her shining armour,

would take me on. As she came — closer, closer — she'd sing, oblivious to my adulation. On the final note of her song, her firm arms would dip and wrap tight around my waist. She'd pick me up from the undergrowth and as I rose my body would give in to her arms, like a marionette to its marionettist.

When she died, I fell from her arms, and when she reached out to catch me it was too late. As I fell, she dissolved. She became the black smoke from the flames that claimed her body. The smoke became thunderclouds. And the clouds gathered — heavy, low. And I ran, again, through the endless field. Above, someone rode with those thunderclouds straddled between their legs. It was Da. But Da did not throw lightning down; Da threw it up, up, up at Ma, who was above us all, somewhere. I kept falling down, down, down from them both. I'd hit the Earth like a meteor. When I did hit, hard, neither dust nor dirt spattered up; rather, Giacomo's laughter rained over all of us, and stung us like the grappa he used to brew at Bete Bolong's prisoner-of-war camp.

The train was rocking and rocking and rocking: a heartbeat, a stomach punch, a pulsing headache. Just rocking. And rocking. Perhaps Morgan would get on the train at the next train stop. I contemplated what could never happen. *Hello*, his familiar voice would interrupt. It would be late. He would sit down across from me; the people in the seats nearby asleep, unlikely to have heard him address me, their pure dreams unmarked by the appearance of such a man sitting, with another man, among them. At peace, unaware, those people held their bags on their laps. They slept, while I looked at the scarf wrapped round his neck and wondered at how the wool's hue enhanced his eyes. I could have leant over and kissed his forehead, so that for a moment he and I would be connected among the masses, the sleeping masses. But then a passenger would awaken, jolted by the sharp movement of the train's carriage. What might happen if the awoken saw one man leaning over to place his lips on the forehead of another man? Would he raise the alarm? Turn away in distaste? Smile in knowing? You couldn't be sure how someone might react. So it was best just to pull your collar up against the side of your cheek, rest your elbow on the window's sill, cover your eyes with your hand, and pretend to be asleep.

Asleep and unaware, no one would wake, no one would raise a knowing smile, curl their lips in distaste, or alarm the other passengers. And because I was asleep and unaware, I'd miss Morgan getting on the carriage. My sleeping lips would never linger on his forehead. He would walk past me because I was an unremarkable mass clumped among the sleeping masses. I suspected that within Morgan ran strong undercurrents. Not so visible from the outside, but I had seen eddies swirl across his façade. I'd later come to know these as his 'sudden silences', suffocated by a change of conversational direction or in the cryptic, coded language we were forced to use. I also had moments like these, which was why I allowed Morgan's currents to drag me down, if only to be closer to a body who, despite what we did not share, had a particular aspect of feeling within the world.

> Dear Morgan,
> I assume you know too well the way
> people can make us feel when we're in
> certain circumstances. Part of me wants to
> blame other people, but I scarcely reach
> out to you because I don't want to face the
> indecisiveness and guilt you arouse in me.
> I *am* indecisive — caught between a world
> that wants people like us to cease and my
> desire to hold you in my arms. I am guilty
> because I'm not sure which of those two
> options is more likely, which of those two
> realities I can commit to. I am this way
> because of how I think of you, and so
> when I do think of you, think of having to
> reply or see to you, I become so guilty. I'd
> rather inflict a wound on myself because at
> least then I would be in control of how it
> affected me.

Dear Christopher,
I'm sitting out on the back step at home,
smoking, thinking about what to write
back to you. A crow perched on the fence,
cawed at me, and spoke to me from a past
place as if to hurry me along. Since the last
time I saw you, you may have changed so
much that I wouldn't recognise you today.
I was pleased to get your letter in the mail,
but the words you wrote didn't convey the
voice I heard when I met you in person.
It felt like getting a letter from the dead.
What is stopping you from speaking? The
longer one suppresses the part of them
that wants to speak, the uglier that voice
becomes as it worms its way underground,
seeking out shadows and always looking
behind. The body above is visible to the
world. The body beneath is visible to only
those that you let in. Let me show you.
Meet me at that quaint coffee shop on
Swanston Street Saturday 3pm.

Saturday came. I awoke before the sun. I shaved and
showered. I brushed sugar-water through my hair,
so that when it dried it stayed in the style I wanted. I
walked back to my bedroom, closed the door. I paced.

The sun rose. From beyond my bedroom walls I heard Kings as he, too, woke, shaved, showered, and dressed. He had breakfast — whistling kettle on the boil, clink of cutlery against china. When he left, the front door banged behind him. And the house fell quiet. And I continued to pace. I had the train schedule memorised. As well as the trams, in case the train had encountered a fault. I knew when each would arrive and when each would open up to the city streets. I knew the path I'd take from the station to the café. But I did not leave the house. I sat on the end of my bed and watched the light change as the sun rose high and then fell. Kings returned after dark. Made some dinner. Listened to the radio, called in another article about a moral crime. He rinsed his dishes, the water splashing into the metal sink. Then he retired, his bedroom door clicking shut.

> Chris,
> I'm beginning to regret writing to you at all. I will not tell you what you already know. I'm not your narrator. You either go after what you can have or you hide because you listen to others saying you can't have it.

> Morgan,
> I don't really expect you to reply to this, and I won't blame you if you don't. The

course of our lives altered when we tripped
over each other. I don't want to belong to
the night anymore. Meet me at Flinders
Street Station on Saturday at 12pm. I hope
we can make our way together.

At the train station, I didn't shake his hand, I didn't say
hello: not because I was concerned by what passers-by
thought of us, but because I felt a greasy unease smeared
over my entire body. I was trying to forge a space free of
men who had well-paid jobs and pretty fiancées, free of
wedding rings and baby bassinets, free of private letters
being stuffed under mattresses or burnt in fireplaces for
fear of what might happen if they were pulled out and
held up in the fierce daylight. Splashed across papers,
rippling through families, like some sort of pestilence.
I did not shake his hand because I could not tell him
that I'd burnt his words in the backyard in the middle of
the night by pouring alcohol over the paper and lighting
them. I'd caught small embers that were tempted to float
away — I didn't want a fire spreading; it must be contained to the house of Christopher. I wanted Morgan.
He shouldn't ever know I'd destroyed his words, but I
wouldn't be surprised to hear that he had done the
same. The only words that remained, the only stories
people would hear, were printed in newspapers and
court reports. I commented on the tailored suit he wore.

Always classy. Sand brown. To reach out and touch its fabric would have been to betray us both.

He said, 'Hello, Christopher,' and suddenly I wished he'd offered to shake.

We'd met at the train station with the intention of taking the train out to the zoo, but when I motioned for us to board he grabbed my arm and asked if I minded if we walked.

I looked at his hand on my forearm. 'The train takes us right beside the zoo.'

'I prefer to walk,' he said.

I stepped back from the train.

He slid his hand back into his own pocket.

We took a path through Melbourne and out onto a wide parade lined with matured oak trees. Full shade. We did not say much. I acquainted myself with the presence of his body beside mine: the length of his stride, his allowing the flies to sit at the corners of his eyes, his bumbling, on occasion, into me.

'You didn't come to the café,' he said. 'I waited for you.'

All I could manage to say was, 'Yes.'

'Why didn't you come?'

I told him I'd got ready and had even planned how I was going to get there. 'I just couldn't stand up from the end of the bed.'

We continued walking. I was unsure if he'd heard what I'd said. Our bodies moved in time with each other's. That road could have stretched forever; I wanted it to stretch forever. At the zoo's entry, we joined the crowd milling through the main gate. Morgan took out from his internal jacket pocket a small drawstring bag, which had cash inside. He held out a note. 'For you to pay.' He slipped the bag away, and I tucked the note into my own jacket pocket.

I went over and bought our tickets.

The salesperson said, 'We've got a rule — one bag of feed per person.' Smile: red lipstick. She handed the bag to me. 'Just remember not to force-feed the animals.'

From the main gate, we moved out into an open area, grassy as if itself a savannah. We walked along a path that ran beside the touring train. Its petite carriages were being loaded with squealing, screeching children; the train was ready to take them to the furthest parts of the zoo, as if the children themselves were exotic creatures being paraded for the caged animals to view. I told Morgan that there was nothing like this in Marlo when I was growing up. 'But would I have been any different to who I am now had I seen a leopard or orangutan as a five-year-old boy?'

He said, 'I don't remember much from before my father brought us to Melbourne, but I do remember it being flat. Land-locked, even though the river was nearby.'

'In Marlo, it felt as if there was more water than land.'

He sniffed, maybe in laughter. 'If it's not too much of one thing then it's too much of another.' He had his hands plugged into his pockets, his wide-brimmed hat tipped low over his face.

The path we walked curved further along to become long, extended, and direct, straight before us, laying out the direction it expected us to take. My shoes scraped the stones on the path, keen to kick up a spray that would rain down miniature meteorites on the couples and young families who splayed picnic rugs across the savannah. Laughing at the caged birds hidden in over-grown aviaries behind them, one of these women rose from her group. Her daughter needed to use the ladies. They walked towards us, she in a white dress, her child in a red dress. She reminded me of Iris; I smiled, but she squinted. She took her daughter's hand, 'C'mon,' and brought the child round to the other side of her body. They took a wide berth on my side.

After they'd passed, Morgan said, 'Why the zoo?' His body drifted a little away from mine.

I picked out a small handful of feed from the paper bag and threw it at a flock of ducks.

'There're too many children, families,' he said.

'But when there's an array of animal oddities for these people to look at,' I whispered, 'two men like us will hardly draw their attention.'

A few yards away stood a short row of rectangular concrete enclosures. Each enclosure had one of its sides cut out and replaced with thick metal bars. Creatures prowled inside where the sunshine didn't fall. A pudding-y kid reached his hand into one of the enclosures. As soon as I could leave Marlo, I had likewise reached for Melbourne. Sick of watching the bruised ocean swell, I fled for Melbourne's streets, its Garden, its men — it all. For fear of being found out. To cover my tracks. Be my own. When, in fact, I was just like that kid leaning over the enclosure's safety barrier, reaching in without understanding what lurked inside.

Morgan said, 'It's not two men together that concerns these people. Not when I'm the man you're with.' He stopped on the path. 'You could be like these people, Christopher.'

'And you?'

'They don't want me to be like them. I don't want to be like them.'

His words prompted me to take his hand and pull him off the main path onto a smaller, sandy path that led through some tall barrier foliage. Sharp bamboo straps sliced our cheeks, our ears. All that glitter, all that gossip, receded as the savannah disappeared behind us.

'Where are we going?' he called from behind.

'Away.'

We sank further into a quieter part.

'From what?'

'Those fucking children and their fucking families.'

Forget forging a normal life: nothing added up

to a whole when you'd been forced to create a bunch of compartments to house your different species. We broke through the other side of the bamboo thicket. We had not fallen into some far-flung Afro-Asian jungle: we'd entered a service alleyway that must have run the perimeter of the zoo. This was where they trucked the shit from the cages to the compost. You could smell it. A lazy afternoon sun, itself done with the day, sank into the space.

He looked up, around. He removed his hat and ran his hand through his hair. As we walked, he fanned his face with his hat.

'My first time,' I told him, 'coming to the zoo — I wanted to be with someone who won't ... Someone who won't mind if I make a fool of myself.'

'I didn't mean coming to the zoo was a bad thing, by the way.'

I nodded.

'Crowds of people like that,' he gestured to the other side of the bamboo barrier. 'One-on-one is what I prefer.'

'I just wanted to share this experience with someone I care for.'

'You could have chosen someone else. That bloke you live with.'

Kings was nothing like Morgan, nor ever would be. And it wasn't because Morgan and I were both *that way*. It was that Morgan had departed from a different starting point to either Kings or me, yet had arrived at the same place as the both of us. There we were, Morgan and I, defying what Kings's newspaper said about us simply by walking down an alleyway at the zoo. In that small, monumental detail there was something worth pursuing.

I said, 'The city always seemed like this magical, different place. But it's much the same here as it is in the country, just bigger and with different street names. When I see Kings kiss Dotty, or she swings her arm round his shoulders, all I think of is having something of my own.' I kicked a length of bamboo that hung into the alleyway. 'A house, an apartment.'

'A place of your own isn't the same as getting away from Kings. Or Dotty. Or the people at this zoo.' He spat air from the side of his lips. 'You'll still be here, in this country, this city, seeing the same people, living between two worlds, living with the same laws.' He stretched his face into the sun, stretched his neck muscles from side to side. 'Despite that,' he exhaled, 'I've always thought I'd go back home.'

'I was so keen to get away from home,' I said, 'but I don't even know what I'm doing here in Melbourne. I dread that I'm running away from something that's already got a hold of me.'

Before he could speak, a whistle, like we were sheep-dogs being called by a sunburnt farmer, pierced into the space. A much taller man, a police officer, was running up behind us. When he got nearer he said, 'Fellas.' In the striking sun, the copper could have been a Hollywood movie star. 'A woman,' he pointed back to from where he had come, 'said she noticed youse coming back here.'

Morgan replaced his hat on his head. 'We're leaving now.'

Copper tucked his thumbs into his belt and sucked on his bottom lip. He stared at Morgan, up and down, as he said, 'You're not meant to be here in the first place.'

'We found ourselves lost,' I said. I looked at Morgan but he did not return my gaze.

Copper said, 'I don't want any trouble.'

Morgan muttered, 'We're on our way out.'

This time Copper's gaze was very much focused on me. 'How d'you know this man?' He nodded at Morgan.

I said, 'He's a friend.'

'Friend?'

Morgan whispered to me, 'Let's just go.' His voice fell into his jacket's weave so Copper didn't hear.

'Family friend.'

'Family?' Copper chuffed. Thumbs still tucked, he stepped closer to me. 'I've cause to question why yer walking down back alleys.'

'As I told you, officer, we found ourselves lost.'

'A vagrant'd say that.' Copper laughed flecks of spit. He pulled out his baton and poked Morgan on the shoulder. 'Got any ID?'

I stepped back a bit from where Copper had accosted Morgan. It was clear that he was not talking to me because he did not look, nor point, nor prod me, nor ask for ID. I asked the officer if he wanted to see my ID, even though I had nothing on me but some cash and an unused train ticket; the officer was uninterested in answering me.

Morgan put one of his hands into his jacket pocket. I couldn't see what he produced for the officer because he positioned his body as if to hide the object from me. Whatever it was, it must have been what the officer wanted. After Morgan replaced it in his jacket, Copper tapped the baton on Morgan's shoulder and told us to move on out of the alleyway.

'If I see youse again in 'ere,' the hoarse voice called, 'even if youse step inside the zoo, I'll string yer up myself.'

When we were back out on the grassy savannah, I said, 'What was that?'

Morgan told me to leave it alone.

'I can't.'

'I'm not asking.' He turned around to face me. Close to me, as close as Copper had got to him. He placed his index finger on my chest and poked me. 'I'm telling you.' Warm air, his breath, fell on me.

The zoo visit was meant to be so raucous, with children chasing pelicans and mothers chasing children and fathers sweating by the snakes, that Morgan and I would be invisible. Our invisibility would have allowed us to wander, to find common ground. But common people — those savannah people — disliked two men like us walking across their ground; even worse, when one of us was even less like them.

'I want to take you someplace,' Morgan called over his shoulder. He was headed for the zoo's exit. He spat onto the savannah as we crossed it.

He took us to a café in the heart of Melbourne. By the time we arrived, it was dusk and the streetlights were beginning to ignite. The café was the one that Jacqui had taken me to. I did not tell him that I'd already been here.

'I stumbled across this place a few years ago,' Morgan said. 'No one asks for ID here.'

He stepped through the doorway, taking hold of the handrail on the wall as if this was his own place. I followed him up. Inside was as I recalled, although louder and with more people. Different people from the last time I was here: all those European gowns had been replaced by people with skin coloured every shade, and mixtures of dress style I'd never known were possible. We found two seats, across from one another, about halfway down the room. The coffee we ordered was cold by the time it got to us. Morgan took one sip, replaced the mug on the table, and pushed it away.

I leant over to say something, but my voice betrayed me; a sharp, crackling pain erupted in my throat when I tried to speak. Similar to when I first arrived in the city and had trouble raising my voice for Kings to hear, I now had trouble raising my voice for Morgan. I avoided those loud places for a reason. I sat back in my chair and drank the cold black liquid.

After the first act, while people were still clapping, a tall, built-up man came over. He squatted. He had a wide grin. He spoke to Morgan. What the two men said was lost in the applause and chatter. The man nodded at me, smiled. I smiled back. He stood up and asked a person beside me if he could take the seat.

After he sat, he introduced himself as Willodee, in a Southern American drawl. 'Y'all not boring him, are you?'

The American appeared quite stern, which made me lose my words. I shrugged.

Willodee said, 'Seems you are.' He held my forearm and squeezed, as if I were a piece of meat he was assessing. He said, 'The look on Morgan's face sticks out like a sore thumb.'

Morgan leant in with his arms on the coffee table and said, 'I'd rather my face looked like a sore thumb than have a face that looked like a—'

'Now y'all tread with care, angel.' Willodee wagged a finger and said to me, 'I'm a former army man. Was based in the Top End for a while there.' He crossed himself: forehead, chest, shoulder, shoulder. He pulled out a chain from round his neck: dog tags.

'My cousin,' I tried to say, 'he tried for years to join.'

'And did he?'

I shook my head. 'Too young.' Simple answers did not express what I wanted to convey, but because of the noise and my uncertain voice, they would have to do.

'And you?'

'Too young, too scared,' I seemed to yell.

'Of?'

'Dying.'

Morgan cut in: 'I wasn't allowed.'

I wanted to contribute. 'Too young?'

He looked across to Willodee, who cocked his head back in my direction. Morgan smirked and dropped his body back into the chair.

Morgan said, 'No, Christopher. It wasn't because I was young.'

'It's because he's half-black,' Willodee chuckled.

'Then how did *you* get in?' I wanted to defend Morgan from what I perceived as a slight from Willodee.

'Who's this bitch?' Willodee laughed. 'Naw, li'l snowflake.' He squeezed my forearm again, harder. 'Black is black.' His voice was lead, dropped heavy on my chest.

'I just meant—'

Morgan leant forward, his hand held out: *stop*. He said, 'Between Willodee and me, black is black. But between you and me, Chris, black can be grey. No one knows what grey means. I fall in the middle of you and him. Willo might not mind me being grey. But to people like you.' He pressed his finger into the table in front of him. 'Walking on this soil.' He jabbed his finger down again. 'I'm suspicious because I'm unclear. Willodee is the night. And you are the day. Me? I'm cloudy. I'm a storm on a summer day.'

Willodee chuckled. 'Y'all gotta stop bringin' in snowflakes, angel.'

I didn't understand.

'If it gets too hot for you,' Morgan explained, 'you'll melt.' In his glance at Willodee, I could tell there was another hidden meaning to the words.

Willodee asked me if I'd been to this café before.

'A few months ago.'

Morgan tilted his head. 'You didn't say.'

'We've all got secrets,' Willodee said. 'So, what do you think?'

'These aren't my people.'

'The crowd changes day to day, night to night. Stick round,' Willodee said, 'an' y'all start thinkin' you've a right to fit with the crowd that lets you fit.'

I said, 'I'm not sure I can stay here.'

Morgan clapped because someone started playing the grand piano on the small stage at the front of the room. Or, perhaps, because he wanted me to stop talking.

I stood. The seat's feet *screak*-ed on the floor.

This noise captured Morgan's attention. He reached out, touched my hand. 'Sit, please. I'm having a good time.'

I didn't answer, nor could I, because a small person had begun singing, and the voice poured inside my chest. I wanted to force it out; it didn't belong there. But I didn't have the lyric with which to sing the tune. I quickstepped out of the room, back down the staircase. Crashed into another quean who was coming up the stairs.

'Are we getting raided, darl?' she cawed with a mouthful of feather boa.

A few days later, I rang Morgan's place. It rang out the first time. I tried again a bit later. A deep, masculine voice answered: 'Forster's.' His father. I slammed the phone down. I stared at it, as if it were that nocturnal demon mære, waiting to climb on me. Then it rang. Electric into my belly. I picked it up. Morgan said, 'I thought it'd be you.'

I asked if he would like to meet me for a coffee in the city. 'Same café, just during the day.'

I decided to walk into the city rather than take a tram or train. A crisp morning, a mid-spring morning. You could feel the sting the sun would deliver later that afternoon, teasing your pale skin. I began going back through the events that had led Morgan and me to this point. I wanted to be sure of things, from my perspective, so I could say to him what I needed to say; I needed him to believe in the truth of the things I was saying.

Whenever we met in daylight, Morgan preferred to walk to wherever we were going. And I didn't mind that: his physicality pushing through space, bumping into me. The officer, believing in his duty, had been so forthright in wanting to see Morgan's identification that day at the zoo; thus, he was presented papers in a back alley, like some underhanded deal. Unlike the mother we'd passed

who'd brought her child in close as if one or both of us were monsters. I'd said nothing to Morgan about her; I'd shoved my hand in the bag of feed like I were the animal it was intended to fill. The suspicious eyed two men walking side-by-side, close enough to brush hands — we both noticed such people. I'd known him to take the night train, the barely peopled train. The quiet train. He was always so quiet. Except in his letters, where his voice soared.

When he'd told me he worked in real-estate maintenance, I had pictured him in vacant houses, his hands recalibrating the interior workings of some or another faulty appliance. He'd been so gentle as he'd taken my hand away from wiping the mud off his lapel — his shoulders dropped, he exhaled, and I could smell on his breath the sweet port I'd watched him drink. I knew he'd expected something else.

By night, the café in the city overflowed with bodies and costumes and light and music. By day, it was unrecognisable. The mauve-painted seating had been replaced with cast-iron garden sets, painted white — two chairs to one small table. At the centre of each was a small crystal vase with some stems and buds. No carpet runner, only the worn-down parquet floor. No standard lamps. Curtains, now opened, allowed warm morning sun to flood the room. Large grey-stone pots, up to my waist, dotted the space and grew *Monstera deliciosa*, *Aspidistra*, *Philodendron*.

A beanstalk boy, unlikely to be eighteen, seated us.

A velvet tuxedo wore him, in that it was so large that he almost disappeared within it. He took our order. His voice was as smooth as the velvet of his suit. No other patrons had yet come out, so Morgan and I were alone. He stroked the broad, shiny leaf of one of the nearby plants. A small slice broke off in his fingers; he dropped it into the pot. The remaining leaf began to weep a white sap. My voice would not betray me this time. No noise or lads to compete with. I would speak without a sharp, crackling pain erupting. I would be heard.

'I've never been here by day,' Morgan said. 'It seems more suitable for you, Christopher.'

I sat back in my chair.

He leant in, his arms on the coffee table, and said, 'I met Willodee when I spent some time in the Top End. The Americans sent a bunch of personnel up there — some strategic bullshit. They never seemed to leave, though.' He pulled out a chain from round his neck: a set of military ID tags. 'Willo introduced me to this guy who'd come over with them,' he said. 'Justin.' He slipped the chain back inside his shirt. 'You tell me you're caught between a world that wants us not to be and your desire to hold me. We have a choice: to accept the world by refusing our desires or to defy that world and take hold of who we are. Justin didn't get that chance. I wear his tags as a reminder of that.'

'I don't know what to do,' I said. 'Each time I get a letter or hear the phone ring. I know what I want to say but as soon as you're around, none of it comes out.'

'You could've written *that* in your letters,' he said. 'You could've said that to me on any of our meetings.'

'I don't know about some things that happen between us — to us — but I know that in your letters you have told me how you feel. You sit here now and speak so confidently. You tell me things that I don't even have the words to describe. I can't always find the words.'

'Show me, then.'

I picked a beach along Port Phillip Bay, which curved round. From the sand you could almost make out where the city may have been: across the bay, it could've been melting in the heat and dissolving in the river, drifting out to sea. A few dinghies had been hauled up out of the sea, bows pressing into the sand. Barnacles on the hulls. Splintered oars tucked under the seats.

I set out the tackle box. Morgan waited, hands on his hips and peering down into its contents.

I swatted at a fly coming towards my eyes. Said, 'Let me show you how I was shown. To hook a worm.' I stood tall behind him and brought my face right beside his cheek; his stubble prickled. I took his hand: soft-skinned, much bigger than mine. I could have raised it and rested his palm on the side of my face. I said, 'I'll hold one of your hands so I can step you through, okay?'

In my other palm was a worm, twisted but placid.

Morgan picked it up when I told him to. Touched and it twirled. When the hook's sharp point pierced through the worm, its skin clicked. Sewerage sludge bubbled. With delicate assurance, I guided his hand holding the worm's body round the hook's bend. Its pink slashed, curled. 'Another loop,' I said, picking up the longer end of the worm and linking it onto the barb. 'And another.' The worm coiled, submitted. 'Hold your rod for a minute,' I instructed. Fossicked among the tussocks in a nearby dune for driftwood and picked up two of similar shape, in a Y, like a slingshot. I drove one stick into the sand, and then did the same with another, placing it close to the first.

Morgan held out his rod as if he were a confused tree.

I asked if he could cast.

He shrugged.

I stood tall behind him again. Walked him closer to the waves. Said, 'With one finger, hold the line on the rod.' I placed my own finger on top of his and pressed the line against the rod. 'Flick the bail.' Which we did. 'Move the rod away from the water — you're going to swing it back to the water in a second and, when it's near the edge, let go of the line. One, two, three.' The rod swayed, Morgan released. The line, led by its heavy sinker, flung out over the rolling waves, landing somewhere between them or beyond them. 'Now flick the bail back to keep the line in place.' He took the rod in both his hands. I picked up my own rod. Repeated the steps

I'd just given. Except when I swung the sinker towards the water, it made a graceful arc before pelleting the ocean. We each placed our rods on one of the Ys and stood, cross-armed, in front of them.

'Watch the tip,' I said. 'If it bends,' I used my arm to demonstrate, 'you've got a fish.

Morgan pointed at his bending rod. 'Like that?'

I leant over and took a hold of the rod. A stressed *click* sounded over and over as I reeled in the line. The tip bent to the surface; I lifted high in the air.

'It'll snap,' he said.

Didn't, though. From the tumbling liquid came a medium-sized fish forged in stainless steel. I grabbed its underbelly. Morgan stepped back with his hands drawn to his chest. The fish appeared lifeless, dripped. Its tail, a film as thin and as beautiful as coloured glass, kicked when I pulled the hook from its fine jawline. A line of bright blood ran round its lips. I dropped the rod on the ground, said to Morgan, 'Watch where you stand — the hook.'

I took out a blade from my trouser pocket.

'Jesus,' he said.

I rested the sharp edge on a small space between the fish's gills. Jerked my arm so the blade sliced into the fish's body. One pulse of blood soaked into the sand. The fish didn't kick.

I re-baited Morgan's hook with another worm and cast the line deep across the swell. He bent over the fish, which lay in a shallow bucket between us.

Grey-water waves curled along the shoreline with a hush and a pause. Against the incessant churning it was hard to tell if the ends of the fishing rods were bending or not. Such uncertainty I'd felt around Da when he took time to do something with me: shooting, fishing. His actions were not unclear; his intentions were. He'd gut the day's catch, yanking out the offal onto the sand and rinsing the fish in salt water. Sometimes with blood still on his fingers he'd re-bait our hooks. Gulls, like maritime vultures, would squabble over the mess he'd left on the beach. Not until Giacomo arrived did I realise a connection between action and intent. As I sat beside Giacomo on the front veranda, I'd watch him line tiny birds' feathers along the shank of a fishing hook. *Pesca*, he'd chuckle, the notes landing on the dusty patch of earth near our feet. He'd hold up the fly he was working on. I hadn't quite grasped what he'd meant until the two of us went fishing one drizzly weekend. A quiet place along the Snowy River, among the bushland. I'd sat down on a rock, damp socking through my shoes. Giacomo was so intricate with the line and the fly flicking on and off the water, dancing. He'd reach out for my hand, helping me up. He'd stand behind me, place the fishing rod in my hands. His huge palms on the top of mine. Wordlessly, he'd move my body to mimic his casting. The fly whipped somewhere overhead.

At home afterward, I prepared the table. Kings and

Dotty were out — at her mother's for the weekend — so we had the place to ourselves. I found in a drawer a red-and-white-chequered cloth, which I draped over the small four-seater table in the dining room. I positioned two candles in two small holders beside each other and then set two plates and two sets of cutlery opposite each other. The ritual laying out of the table was somehow religious. I said, 'Did you have to read the Bible at school?'

He hummed a yes or a no.

'Once when it was my turn to read, I fainted — it was bloody hot, I tell you. I hadn't eaten. But the teacher thought I was possessed or something. I had to go to see the priest. I said into the confessional mesh, *my teacher sent me to you.* To which Father replied, *and there is nothing more I can help you with.*'

Morgan said, 'I suppose you could have been possessed.'

'Possessed with a knowledge that they didn't want me reading from the Bible. So, I wrote a poem about the end of the world as penance.' I turned away. 'I'll gut the fish.'

I didn't tell him that my fainting was after I'd seen Kings's *things* — everything had begun to overwhelm me but I had no one to whom I could express myself. My words had dissolved in the acids of my stomach. I'd lost the ability to speak.

I placed the blunt edge of the knife against the

fish's scales; the body dipped where the blade pressed, accommodating my task. I scraped along the shiny body, moving the knife away from myself in a firm and smooth line. The blade undid the interlocked scales.

'I never did anything like this,' Morgan said, 'at the boys' home.' That's where he had lived before his father came to get him. 'Just like an orphanage,' he said, 'though filled with kids whose families were still alive.'

'Why were you there?'

'They wanted us to be with the right family. Taught us how to fit in.'

'With what?'

'With people like you.' He played with some of the scales I'd taken off the fish. Rubbed them between his fingers.

I hadn't been paying attention to what I was doing — I'd glanced at him and the blade slipped. 'Fuck!' I dropped the knife, which spun from the chopping board and clanged down into the sink. 'I cut my finger.' I pushed him aside so I could wash it under the tap.

His hand brushed my back. 'Do you have any bandages?' I gestured to a drawer, which he opened. He took out a rolled-up length of white bandage. 'Dry your hand.' He unwrapped the material. When my hand was dry, he took it in his. Folded over the end of the bandage and placed it on the cut, which wasn't that deep. He bound the material tight. 'You have scissors?'

I nodded. 'Up this end.'

We shuffled to a far-end drawer. He held the bandage and my finger, and I held out my free hand, ready to clasp the drawer handle. I pulled out a pair of scissors. He cut the bandage. I put the scissors away. He used a metal pin to hold the bandage in place.

I returned to the chopping block, my back to him. I reclaimed the knife. I rested its tip on the fish's anus. Drew the blade through the flesh of its belly, up to under its jaw. When the cut was made, I placed the knife aside. There was a patch of red on my bandage now, faint enough that I convinced myself it was my own blood. I tucked a thumb inside the fish's mouth and dragged my unbandaged hand through its belly. The internal organs sucked against each other, snapped, protested at being removed. I pulled them all out, dumping the inedible offal in the sink, and rinsed the fish's internal cavity under running water. Little clots of blood rushed away from its rib cage. I shook the excess water off, then placed the carcass aside. I bagged and discarded the offal and scales. Returned to the fish. Its eyes clouded over.

I said, 'What else did you do learn at the boys' home?'

He was standing close beside me, watching. 'How to be unseen and unheard. How to be seen and heard.'

As I prepared the fish for cooking, I said, 'I thought all children were taught that?'

Then Morgan stopped me. 'What are you doing it like that for?'

'It's how you cook it.' Gutted fish on foil with oil, salt, pepper, lemon.

He made a move to pick up the fish. I asked what he thought he was doing, swatted his hand.

'Let me show you how I was shown,' he said, 'a new way.'

'This is how I've always done it.'

'And it doesn't make it wrong,' he smiled at me, 'but it doesn't mean it's the only way.' He picked up the fish from the tray I'd prepared it on. He washed it under the tap, washed all the oil, salt, pepper, lemon down the sink. He re-laid the tray with clean foil and put the fish on top. He squeezed a lemon over it. 'I might not have learnt how to fish or to clean one, but I *did* learn how to cook,' he said. He motioned us outside. On a patch of dirt in the backyard, he cleared a small patch of ground. When he was satisfied, he stood tall and instructed me to help collect twigs and dry grass to place there. He broke the twigs up into manageable pieces. He laid a foundation of tinder, over the top of which he built a teepee from larger sticks. He lit the fire, blew gently to excite the flame. He said we'd have to build up the coals a bit first, but that it wouldn't take long. Red-hot coals would be the best way of cooking the fish. He kept stoking the fire, building a pile of coals.

'My mother used to do this,' I said, 'when she boiled billy tea.'

'Never with fish? Meat?'

'Ma always cooked meat in a pan over flame.'

When there were no longer any flames, he said it was ready. He laid the foiled fish on top of the embers. 'Five or so minutes either side,' he said. 'Can you do the veg? Just steam them. Not much — don't want them soggy.'

I made my way back inside to steam carrot, squash, and beans. I laid them out on the two plates.

He came in behind me, rubbed his hands on his pants. He picked up the two plates I'd served with veg and told me to come back out to the fire's side. He'd removed the fish from the coals and rebuilt the fire so it was burning low.

'Are you sure it's cooked?' I sat one side of the fire and he on the other.

He placed our plates on the grass. Unwrapped the foil. A plume of blue steam rose. With a fork, he broke the flesh away: firm, glossy, white. Served us equal shares beside the veg. When he was done, he handed over my plate and took up his own. Soft fish flesh broke easily under his teeth.

We'd been spending more time together. There *were* opportunities for us to meet at Kings's, but such times were few and far between — they were precious. When we could not meet there, we walked beside each other. Sometimes chatting, sometimes quiet. Sometimes we'd end up back in the city. And our lips would come undone.

He told me my skin was soft under certain lights. I told him I washed almost every day. He smiled and told me he liked to see my softness.

And I asked him, 'Why?'

He told me that it gave him hope that in time, in the daylight, I'd show someone besides him what softness I have for him. And I told him that he was the only person who mattered; he was the only person who needed to know.

He told me that I had to tell someone. 'Because if you don't tell someone about me, then I'll always just be a no one.'

I changed the subject. I told him about how Ma's hands used to rub talcum powder between my toes after a bath. How soft, how smooth. 'I'd giggle and wriggle, and she'd sing *this little piggy went to market*.' He told me about the first time his father came for him at the boys' home. How he'd stood in the doorway of the dormitory, tall and shadowy. He told me that even though he hadn't seen his father's face, he'd been torn between leaving the boys he'd been sleeping, eating, learning, and being beaten alongside and going away with the only person he'd been told was family.

'Turns out I had no choice,' he told me. 'I was being taken away — again.' He reached out for the wine, grabbing the bottle by the neck. As he lifted it to his glass, it fell, like a slick of oil, from his grip and smashed on the floor. 'Shit.' He flicked his hand, wiped the residue on his pants.

'Here' — I went to help pick up the mess — 'I'll help.'

He batted me away. 'I'm able,' he told me. He knelt on one knee beside the mess and extracted shards of glass from the spreading pool of wine. He piled these in his cupped palm, curling his fingers, his flesh, round the slicing edges.

I went to take the shards from him, but again he stopped me; his grip tightened instead. I knelt down, too, and took his hand in mine. 'You'll cut yourself,' I told him. I lifted his fingers. I picked out what broken glass he held and placed it into my own palm.

In the shower, I checked his arms for self-inflicted scars or marks. He could have the same thoughts as me. As he was washing, water ran over his closed eyes and his hands rubbed at his face. He did not have a blemish, but I determined he carried them within. What reason did he have to show them? In those early days I thought I did a pretty good job of not showing him mine, though they did sometimes bob up, as if a silky cormorant resurfacing with a bellyful.

I anticipated our bodies coming together; our bodies expected it. We had held back the urge. Until, when the evening had died and the neighbourhood had fallen silent, there was, in that silent darkness, his hand; silent, until it rustled on my thigh. I gasped. *Shush*. And I shushed. It continued to happen, again, and then again, and then I lost count. He stayed on top of me after he was done, chest panting onto mine until it settled. He kissed, always. He made sure the bedsheets covered me, even if that meant they didn't cover his body as well. I forgot that I was expecting anything. I began to enjoy what we were doing, the feel of his body on and inside me. And sometimes it was me who was on top of him. And it was me who folded down so that my chest panted onto his. And I, too, never rolled. I kissed him. Then pulled the bedsheets over him; I, however, always kept enough to cover myself, too. A difference in approach. Then we slept. And in the morning, before the world was clear-eyed, we would go, quiet, to our days.

He did not know what my day, hour by hour, consisted of, and nor did I know how his was structured. I'd imagine him standing in some stranger's house — called out to repair a leaky toilet or re-hinge a faulty door. At his maintenance work. Sometime afterward, standing in a stranger's house as the sun came through the lace.

I became a buffoon, so enamoured that I reverted to a clumsy teenager: I was that boy who had run home after seeing another boy's things only to find my hairless own. Morgan appeared too caught up in his own vast interior to fully notice me, so I focused on my protective adoration, which was pleasant, suffocating, and swung between being a necessity and a commodity. Exhausting. *Come here, I need you. Get away, my skin's crawling*. But in that *get away* — more often seeping from his lips, his fingertips — it was the buffoon in me that pawed back at him, at the world. Morgan prowled the boundary. 'It's like having a barnacle attached to my side,' he'd joke. But there was little I could say to that, except, 'I enjoy your company.'

In the 1950s I could have bought a house for £1,000, more or less, but I was a junior mechanic earning £5/15s a week; I could only imagine having enough to afford a terrace or flat by placing some lucky bet trackside. So I'd organised an appointment with a real estate agent to show me some rental properties one Saturday morning. I was used to paying a pittance to stay with Kings. The agent wasn't all that keen, but I told him some bull about wanting a place, short-term, that'd tide me over until I bought a house of my own. I hadn't shared my decision to move out with Kings or Dotty. They had their own lives they were concerning themselves with.

The house was narrow, brick-veneer. Detached. With a front yard full of trees and flowerbeds planted with geraniums, a silver birch, wisteria, a gum, and daisies and daisies and daisies. Agent closed the front door: behind the heavy timber, the sound from outside did not carry. The first door on the right opened into the front room, which was rather plain, with a fireplace across from the door, and, at the top of the room, a bay window with fine lace draped on the inside. From here you walked down the hallway, passing through a set of sliding doors into a scullery, which in turn led out into an elongated court-yard that backed onto a laneway. There was enough room to populate the yard with small shrubs, to host barbeques, to throw a summer picnic with all sorts. I imagined Morgan standing in the centre of the courtyard, holding a jar of hooch. He was talking to Willodee and Jacqui; the former dressed in a fine Italian tux, the latter in a ball gown of green. Tall trees arched overhead, creating an intricate, impenetrable cage for us all. There were other people, too, who held shallow champagne glasses (the kind moulded from Marie Antoinette's breast). From where these people stood, they pointed to the fairy lights hung in the canopy-cage above, which twinkled and created our own form of heaven.

Back inside and up the main hallway were two doors into the two bedrooms, each with a small fireplace of its own. In the larger bedroom at the front of the house, I stood under a cast-iron chandelier. Sun sparked off its crystal pendants. Rainbow flecks scattered my face. There was enough room in the main bedroom to put a wide bed, with white sheets and a black iron frame to match the chandelier. A rug, Egyptian, underneath so that our feet did not get cold on the winter floorboards. We'd buy a kitchen table to pass on to our next generation. Even get a cat. Our cat. We'd call it Tabby (although she'd be more a tortoiseshell). We'd let her sleep between us, at risk of being crushed when one of us rolled over in the night. In time, and after many courtyard parties, she'd grow as we fed her diced heart and liver or the offal from gutted fish. She'd bring mice home as a gifts of thanks, the guts smeared red on our doormat. She'd stop snakes in their tracks before one of us found them slinking in the scullery. One of us would clean her tiny turds from the garden beds while the other moaned about the noxious scent of her shit. But when she grew older, when she developed a kidney dysfunction, we'd still let her rest between us on our bed despite her incontinence. And we'd like to be, when the time came, as heroic as to drown her rather than hear her day by day weaken, weaken, and stop eating.

On moving day, the terrace house I'd leased echoed without anything being said inside it. I stretched my hands overhead, arched my back and yawned. I wanted to walk around in my Y-fronts, to eat breakfast for dinner, to lay my hands all over Morgan's body. There was something about the house's size, about the way the roof extended so far out of reach that I could hardly see its edges, that allowed me to breathe. We brought in the few boxes and items of furniture I'd gathered over the years. We laid them out. He'd suggest placing something one way, I'd suggest the other; we'd natter till we found a compromise.

I continued unpacking alone. I played the wireless as I went, and when I was done I began to decorate the house for Christmas, just around the corner. Earlier on that day, on one of the trips between Kings's and the new house, I had made Morgan pull over beside a railway line so that I could dig up a tree that'd been growing between the tracks. When Morgan visited next, he stood back from the now decorated tree. Could have been pine, could have been anything; it fit what I thought a Christmas tree ought to look like. Wispy fronds reached a few centimetres above my knees. Table-top height. It was adorned with a mimicry of what Iris once made: a garland of white-fabric ribbons fastened to twine and paper cut-outs of snowflakes and snowmen and candy canes.

'Surprise,' I said to Morgan. 'There were meant to be candles round the base but the flames reached too high, and I didn't want to burn down the house.'

He said, 'At least the tree would be gone.' He rubbed its foliage between his fingers and sniffed the residue. 'Why pine?'

'What else would it be?'

'Anything,' he said, 'nothing.' He took a paper snowflake in his hand, slid it off the branch, and hung it from his finger. He held his hand out, palm flat, so the ornament swayed aloft. 'What does a snowflake mean to me when I've never seen snow?'

'My sister used to make them for the tree we had as kids,' I told him.

'And what species of tree was that?'

I shrugged. 'Eucalypt?'

He put the ornament down on the coffee table. 'Are

you happy with this tree, Christopher?'

Lush green with stark white decorations.

'It's neat,' I said with a smile.

'I'm glad that you are happy.'

I asked if he liked it.

'It's your home,' he said, 'so it only matters that you do.'

I picked up the ornament and replaced it from where he had removed it.

He did not stay for dinner that night, nor on any of the nights in the week leading up to Christmas Day. When I asked him if he'd make time to have a late-night Christmas drink with me, he seemed to choke on his tongue.

'You don't have to,' I conceded. 'I'm just putting the offer out.' In fact, I had placed an order for an extra cut of rabbit, stocked up on wine, and got more mince pies than two people would ever need.

'Would you mind,' he said, 'if I stayed the whole weekend?'

I froze. 'Won't your father mind?'

'He'll have his own family with him on the day,' he said and kissed me on the cheek.

After all that, Christmas Eve settled in. I sat down on the veranda with a glass of wine. Black sky, stars through the leaves of the gum. Morgan's heavy feet, inside the house, came closer to the door. We were night-creatures. We had a routine of arriving under the cover of night, of leaving before first light, of secret houses and telling stories to pass the time before we could see each other again. It was a constant furling-unfurling of a spring-time soft bud. Except we were flowers on a shrub hidden at the bottom of the garden. We were plains wanderers. Morgan took a spot beside me. He put two plates of Christmas dinner — rabbit, spuds, mushrooms — between us. He ran back inside to retrieve two jars of hooch, which he had brewed.

'One for you,' he said, placing a jar between my feet, 'and one for me.' He twisted open the lid of his, held it up. 'Cheers.'

I did the same. Cricket chirrups ricocheted off our swallowing necks. Mosquitoes bit exposed skin.

'I used to play this game as a little boy,' he said after a while. 'I'd hide under the bed when there were thunder-storms — I thought the thunder was a pair of enormous fists belting on the roof.' He forked a field mushroom but did not eat. 'I'd lie there under the bed, eyes squeezed closed.' He demonstrated what he meant. 'I'd pretend a wall divided my room in two halves. And there was one person standing in each half of the room. Two people I cared about. And I was on the outside of the room, looking in.'

Summer night lethargy: our two bodies, so close, created inhumane heat; my heartbeat pumped magma.

'A whitewashed room,' he said, 'brickwork painted over. The room appeared endless.' He stroked his hair. 'At the other end of the room I could see a silhouette holding a gun.'

'This is morbid.'

He laughed or coughed in his mouth. 'I also had a gun,' he said. 'Each time thunder cracked, I pulled the trigger.' He did not tell me who he had shot at: the ones he loved, the silhouette, himself. He said, 'It gave me hope that I might have a long-lost twin I'd one day need to fight for.' He sighed. 'I want you to know something about me.' He reached into his back pocket and pulled out a folded piece of paper. He handed it to me to unfold.

> **Certificate of Exemption**
> **Aborigines Protection Act**
> This to certify that you are a person
> who, in the opinion of the Board for
> the Protection of Aborigines, ought no
> longer be subject to the provisions of the
> Aborigines Protection Act and regarded
> as a citizen of the ordinary community.
> This certificate may be revoked at any
> time and without warning by the Minister
> administering the Act.

'It's what we call a dog tag,' he said.

I turned over the paper to see what was on the other side, but it was blank.

'It's what I showed that copper at the zoo,' he said. 'Never had to show it before, but. It's meant to help me to get around without trouble. Part of the reason we moved down here, to get away from dog tags and what not. Always thought it was a bit of a laugh when I was a boy.'

'Where did you get it from?'

He swigged the hooch before he took the dog tag back from me. 'From the home I grew up in. It's a New South thing, though. Not Vic. All us boys up there got one.' Refolding it, he said, 'Everyone bothers over our looks,' he flashed the folded paper as an example, 'so they don't think about anything else. Such as who I'm spending all my time with.' He drank again. 'And I like that — being able to keep some parts of myself to myself. Only showing those parts on my terms. While I might not always feel like that, it's how I feel for now.'

When I woke, he was holding me from behind. His warm breath blowing on my neck. Long, deep inhalations, slow, drawn-out exhalations. I curled my body, closer, into his shape.

The first knock on the front door was very firm.

'Expecting visitors?' Morgan said.

'No,' I whispered.

He let go of me. 'Who could it be?'

I sat up, and moved to the side of the bed.

The second knock, preceded by a hesitant pause, was much less sure.

I stood up and put my underwear on. 'Stay here,'

I told him. I cleared my throat as I walked down the hallway. I puffed my chest and angled my feet outwards, so my gait was more masculine, more forward. Expect the worst, prepare for the worst. Perhaps the neighbour had lost their dog. Perhaps I'd forgotten to leave out the crate for the milkman. I opened the door.

'Kings?'

He was dressed in a short-sleeve shirt, linen shorts, and tan leather slip-ons. 'Sorry,' he said, 'I must have woken you.' He glanced down at my underwear. 'I've just come to—'

'Who is it, Chris?' Morgan had come down the hallway. He placed his palm on the small of my back, out of sight. He wore only underwear, too.

'This is Kings,' I told Morgan. 'I used to live with him.'

Morgan leant round me, held out his hand, and introduced himself. 'I've heard so much about you.'

'You've company,' Kings said. 'I didn't realise. I just came to drop off this letter. It's postmarked Marlo.'

Because Kings had not shaken his hand, Morgan took the letter. 'I'll put this away,' he told me and walked back down the hall.

Kings: broad-shouldered, blond hair, twinkling eyes. An advertisement. A film star. A boy who'd stopped in the middle of a paddock, fingers at his fly, ready to show you the hairs growing round his things. A man who'd let you live with him as his own life grew. He half-smiled.

Said, 'Might see you around.'

I closed the door. Morgan had left the letter on the hall stand. I collected it and returned to bed where he was, tucked up under the duvet. A letter from Iris, dated recently. I ran my finger under the flap and ripped it open.

'She's being married,' I said. 'My sister.'

'You sound stunned.'

'I haven't spoken to her in such a long time. I just …' I showed him the letter. 'I knew it was coming,' I told him. 'She's been going with that bloke for a while, I just … didn't expect it to happen so soon.'

We placed our travel cases in the overhead rails and took a seat opposite each other. I ran my hand over the leather upholstery of the train carriage. Morgan had been hesitant in agreeing to come to Iris's wedding. I'd assured him — of what, I wasn't sure: safety, fun, protection, family? Perhaps he agreed because he felt obliged. The train lurched away from the platform. As we sat down, a gush of steam billowed and filled the window. Under the cover the white-grey plume provided us, I leant across and kissed his lips.

*

The Orbost valley was covered by hundreds of acres of maize crops. We'd passed along many sleek herds of cows gathered round the milking yards late in the afternoon. As we descended the valley, the memory of people who had departed flicked like passing trees, blurry but visible enough to leave an impression.

Iris answered the door; flung it back so hard it dented the wood panelling on the wall. She had curlers in her hair, a dressing-gown wrapped round her body. She hugged down my arms and I couldn't hug her back. 'I was sure you'd miss the train,' she said.

I lifted my travel case and crossed the doorway into the house. 'I'd never,' I said, 'not when my sister's getting married.'

'I don't feel like that.' She rubbed her forearm.

'How do you feel?'

'Alone,' she moaned. Then, looking beyond me, 'I see *you're* not alone.'

I turned to introduce him to her.

Morgan held out his hand. She shook it.

She said, 'What are you doing here?'

'For your wedding.'

'My wedding?'

Morgan held his travel case handle with both hands in front of him.

She seemed to be waiting for me to look at her, to make eye contact, but as I spoke I continued to look at Morgan, as if addressing him.

'You told me in your letter that you'd like me to bring someone.' I asked Morgan to come up inside and put his bag away. He took his shoes and hat off outside the door. He walked through the gap between Iris and me, down the hall and into my old bedroom, as I'd directed.

Iris touched my arm when he was out of view. She brought her mouth in close to my ear and her warm breath said, 'You brought a man.' She let go of me. 'A *dark* man.'

'I didn't *bring* him,' I said. 'I wanted him to come. I asked and he said yes.'

She peered down the hall where Morgan had disappeared and said, 'Just be glad Da's not home.'

We went into my old bedroom. Morgan was unpacking from his travel case a pair of PJs. He laid them out on the bed, ready for when he'd be sleeping.

Iris said, 'You can put your things in the tallboy.' She pointed. 'If you prefer.'

'Thanks,' he said, 'but I like to keep my things together.'

I undid my own case on my old bed. I took out my clothes, meaning to put them into the tallboy as she had suggested, but when I saw my shirts — clean-starched and ironed — resting against the washed-out linen the bed was made up in, I replaced them in my case and slid the whole thing aside: past did not sit harmoniously beside present. Iris sat on the end of my bed. She watched Morgan fiddle with some bits and pieces inside his travel case. He turned, noticed her, and laughed in an uncertain way. She laughed likewise, and then turned to me.

I said, hands on my hips, 'Do you have a picture of the man you're being given away to?'

She tutted. 'He's not posh, if that's what you mean.'

I thought of the picnic I had gone to with Kings and Dotty, and how one of the others there had been snapping shots of us all afternoon. I said, 'Having a camera doesn't make one posh.'

'Saying *one* does,' she said.

I said dumbly, 'One has still not seen who's stealing one.'

'The man who is stealing me is not like the city,' she said, 'which stole you.'

'The city doesn't steal,' Morgan said, 'it swallows.'

Iris considered his words. She said, 'It all happened very quickly.'

'The wedding?' I asked.

'Well ... everything,' she almost whispered.

I glanced at Morgan. He was taking out a pair of running shoes and a set of clothes. I said to my sister, 'Where will you be spending your honeymoon?'

She crossed her arms. 'We don't have the money for anything special.'

'A honeymoon is a waste of money,' Morgan said. 'You return home only to work in order to pay back the pleasure.'

Iris said, 'I do enough work as it is.'

'Precisely,' he said. 'Excuse me while I get changed.'

'Where are you going?' she said.

'For a run.' He went out into the hall; his bare feet stepped away, then a door, the bathroom door, clicked shut.

'A run?' she asked me.

'Clears his head.'

'He just got here.'

'He likes to run.'

She stood up and went over to Morgan's travel case. Her fingertips brushed against it — the top lid was closed, but not locked. She checked over her shoulder to make sure he had not returned before lifting the lid.

'Iris,' I scolded.

She hummed. She held the lid aloft and, with her other hand, touched Morgan's items within.

'What are you doing?' I went from her to the door. I clutched the jamb, popped my head round into the hall. Nothing.

Back in the room, she had opened the travel case so far that the top now lay flat on the bed. She held a small rectangular box in both hands. The bottom was plain-brown cardboard, the lid wrapped in a blue-paisley paper.

Down the hall, the bathroom's door opened.

'Iris.' I went to her. I wanted to whack the box from her hands and flip the travel case closed, but she was holding the box, caressing it. Morgan was so particular with his things that he'd notice even a misplaced crease in his folded trousers.

She said, 'Do all men have a little box like this?'

Steps: closer, closer.

I snatched the box from my sister. She stepped out of the way. As I was replacing the box under one of Morgan's shirts, he came in and asked me what it was that I was doing. I closed the lid. When I turned, I met Morgan's gaze.

He was still out for a run by the time I was getting ready for bed — possibly running back to Melbourne. I made my way into the bathroom, intending to brush my teeth and scrub my face. I found Iris in front of the vanity's mirror. She dropped one of her hands from her face when I walked in. Sniffed. I asked if she was okay. She smiled to my reflection and picked up her toothbrush, confirming that she was just getting ready for bed. She should have been surrounded by maternal grace, by sororal links from her school days; friends, and friends of friends, and aunts caressing her, brushing her hair for her. A mother to oversee, to set the expectations. All the women had gone. It was the night before her wedding, yet there she was in the bathroom being interrupted by her brother; that was as bad as the groom seeing his bride on the morning of the ceremony. A few flecks of white flicked out of her mouth as she brushed her teeth. Her other hand rested on her belly.

She'd always been beside me. In her lacy Sunday

dresses, running through the apple orchard out the back of the church. She was faster, so I was the one that our Sunday-school teacher saw dash into the trees. I was the one that, later on, got into trouble. She'd wait for me afterward, squatting over some monstrous bull-ant mound while poking a stick into its entrance. Infuriated pincers lashed beneath her yet she managed never to be bitten; somehow, she'd discovered a foolproof method. She forever knew multitudes. And she didn't need a box to keep her secrets in: she was a vault herself. There'd be no hands lifting her out from a travel case, turning her to see her from different angles. She had no lid, no hinge. Four elements held her together: *maintain, hold yourself, be present, be available*. She, like me, had begun in our mother. When she came out, her feminine mould determined the shape of her life. She was to uphold and administer a daily routine. Nothing — not the harshest statement or the rawest emotion — seemed as bitter to her child-self than waking in winter before dawn. Some mornings she'd touch me and I was sure there was frost on her skin. Feeling around in the darkness for a candle to light, she could've fallen off the edge of the world. But then the flame ignited and the world came into sight. Each list of tasks seemed impossible; the repetition of each day became a hymn, timed by the passing hands of a hallway clock. She'd be at some task — scrub floor, hang washing, kindle fire — when our mother passed and clipped her ear. *Lift from the chest; don't hang off your spine.*

I said, 'You've come so far.'

She scoffed through the foam, and hawked into the basin. Foamy lips spoke, her voice resounding off the water's running tap. 'And what've I got to show for it?'

'A confidence that would frighten our mother.'

She spat out the toothpaste, washed the residue from her mouth. She replaced her brush in a rather filthy glass on the basin.

I mentioned Morgan's case. 'Just because he's not like you doesn't mean you can go through his things.'

'You're right.' She turned and crossed her arms. 'But Morgan is no different to, I don't know, Da or Giacomo. More importantly,' she stressed, 'Morgan is no different to you.'

'I don't understand.'

'You're all men.' She turned to the mirror, ran her fingers through her hair. 'And men, by nature, have trouble communicating.'

Without brushing my own teeth, I left her there.

The door of the bedroom was closed, the pale wood scratched and dented. The room had once smelled of life; precisely, the body odour of two teenaged boys, mine and cousin Jimmy's. Inside was dim. A thin sheet of grey material draped over the only window created a suspicious light. There were two beds: mine from when I was a boy and another, which had belonged to Jimmy. He'd moved in after his mother absconded — we later found out she'd left after receiving a telegram telling her that her husband was missing, presumed dead, in the war. The space at the end of mine and Jimmy's old beds appeared much tighter, more awkward, than I remembered. As a smaller child, that space between the end of my old bed and Jimmy's, which pressed up against the wall under the window, was as long as forever; even if I jumped, I wouldn't have made it across the gap. But now, years after I'd last slept in here, my old bed seemed to carve into the side of Jimmy's. Inseparable. One car T-boning another.

Morgan would be sleeping in Jimmy's bed tonight. On the wall opposite the door was the tallboy. I'd once watched Jimmy unpack his undies into it; that was the day he moved in. I was worried that by keeping our undies in the same drawer we'd mix them up and wear a pair of the other's, but Jimmy told me that wouldn't matter because we were both boys. On top of the tallboy, still, were the few trinkets my cousin brought with him: a small toy soldier (which he used to hold close to his head every night when he slept), my old copy of *El Loro*, and a chain of rosary. *Shush*. There cousin Jimmy was, straddling me in my bed. His thighs tight over my waist as he pressed his pelvis down into me. I ran my hand over the sheets. Safe — that's what I had felt with his body weight holding me down. But I attempted to wriggle, if only (I wondered now) to engage my body with his broader, stronger body. I pulled back the sheets and fluffed the pillow. His thighs tight against my body.

His hand very gentle on my mouth. His nose against my nose. I slipped in underneath. We looked into each other's eyes: his were dark, but I saw a speck of light reflecting on the bulb. I covered myself. He placed his lips on my forehead. Lingered.

The bedroom door opened, the light switched on: Morgan.

He said, 'I thought you'd be with your sister.'

'She went to bed,' I said.

He came in and took off his sweaty shirt, hung it over the cast-iron bed frame as if to air it. Bare-chested. He sat down on the side of his bed to undo his shoelaces. His shoulders rotated.

I sat up in bed and ran my hands through my hair before I said to him, 'About your travel case.'

He lifted one of his feet up onto the opposite thigh and pulled off a running shoe, then a sock. When he bent his toes, the joints cracked loud. He did the same with his other foot. Stood and stretched his hands high above his head. As he bent down to pick up both shoes and socks, he said, 'Rifling through my things?' He lined up his shoes at the end of the bed and laid out each sock on top of each shoe. 'A mate of mine gave me that box a few years back.' He undid his flies with one hand, slid his running shorts off to reveal grey underwear. 'Same mate I used to live with at the boys' home.' Sweat patches round his groin made the material darker in those places. He hung the shorts beside his shirt on the bed frame.

Another sweat patch lined his arse. 'That box,' he said, 'it's got a bunch of stuff in it from when he and I were in the boys' home together.' He took off his underwear, smelled it, and pulled away. He hung that, too, alongside the shorts and shirt on the bed frame. He put on a long pair of PJ bottoms. He faced me. 'You needed to ask me if you wanted to look at it.'

'I didn't know it was there.'

Morgan reached into his travel case and retrieved the box. Held it out, arm stretched, to me. 'I've already shown you my dog tag,' he rattled the box, 'so now you can see what that means to me.'

'I shouldn't have seen it in the first place. Not without you here.'

'I'm here now.' He kept the box there for a bit, but then pulled it away. Replaced it in his case, under his clothes. He closed the lid and locked it before sliding the whole thing under his bed and switching off the bedroom light.

Da sat in the very first pew, directly in front of me, but didn't say a word to me. When he'd walked in, he'd kept his eyes down, not even acknowledging Lowell, Iris's groom, who stood before the altar. I watched a bead of sweat slide down the back of Da's neck. Iris's dress was full round her body: skirt down to her ankles, rounded shoulders, higher-than-usual neckline. She could be a sister committing herself to god. In her flat shoes, unfavourably beige, she faced her dapper bridegroom in his second-hand suit. Together they repeated verbatim what Father Poltrone said. Her nervous husband lifted the veil and pressed his face onto hers. I glanced at Morgan: a seraph in the lemon-hued sunlight, placed as if he'd always been here.

Most receptions down in Marlo were held in the RSL Hall, and Iris's was no exception. Morgan and I stood outside in the dark after all others had gone inside. He turned away from the light that issued from the hall's wide windows.

'That first time you and I met,' he said, 'I wasn't there for that reception. I didn't even know who was being married. I knew you were following me. I was glad I tripped over you and got mud all over me. I didn't think I'd ever see you again, then you invited me on the train ride home — and, well, I couldn't say no.'

'You can always say no.'

He stepped in a half-circle. 'I might be able to say no to you. I can't say no to the rest of your kind.'

'Is this about what Willodee was saying?'

'Yes. No.' He threw one hand up. 'I don't know.'

I scratched the side of my head. 'I'm not sure what to say, Morgan.'

'I don't know if there's anything you *can* say right now.'

So I didn't.

'I can't go in there.'

And again I did not speak.

He sighed, said, 'I'll see you back at the house.'

I couldn't follow him home. It was Iris's wedding and I'd already taken so much from her: her dream of moving to Melbourne, her brother, her family. I looked back at Morgan. His body, by this time, was no longer visible in the darkness. He had been more forthcoming than I had. He'd chosen to show me his certificate of exemption. I had seen what he'd not wanted me to see — that blue-paisley box. Despite this betrayal, he had shared with me where that box came from, all while he had stripped himself naked. I'd not looked inside it because I was embarrassed.

I went inside. I found a crystal punchbowl twice the size of a human head sitting centre of table at the back of the room. I had my back turned to where the tables stood, like stagnant dancers on an unswaying dancefloor. I picked up the silver ladle and tipped the strawberry-coloured liquid into a tumbler. I turned, with my tumbler, and wandered through the crowd of people. Skolled the liquid and left the glass on a table at the side.

Iris rested her head on the shoulder of her husband, Lowell, as they danced. Tall, much taller than me, and with blue eyes the colour of swimming-pool water, Lowell was a wedge-tailed eagle in an empty sky, eyeing his prey in the strappy grass. He was a different kind of man to that of my father. Da was silent, stoic, from a generation of men who'd absorbed war and the Depression into their souls and were then left speechless at having to carry the weight of those experiences. He seemed to accept his lot in life. Any improvement was undeserved; any displeasure was the result of having wanted or accepted more. Perhaps that's why he was absent from the reception. Lowell, similar in age to me, had missed having to participate in war. As for the Depression, while we didn't know any different, any improvement felt like winning the lottery. We knew things *could* get better and so we found ways to try to make them better.

When the band finished the song, Iris dipped away from Lowell and placed a hand against her belly. Everyone clapped for the musicians. When she saw me, her shoulders relaxed. She twirled me in for a dance. She placed the side of her face against my chest, though I'd wanted to place mine on her chest. The music was fast enough for those swivelling, Charleston-like pivots, but Iris was in control — the lead — and kept us in a steady, slow-waltzing pace from a quieter time.

'You saved me,' I said.

'You don't seem to need me anymore. You have Morgan.'

I cleared my throat.

'Who is he, Chrissy?'

'He's Morgan.'

'Who is he to you?'

I batted away her questions, her unspoken accusation, because I didn't want to make a scene. 'Tonight's about you,' I said.

'It stopped being about me when you brought him,' she said.

Even if I had come alone, even if I had sat in the front row at church, these people would not have greeted me, would not have asked what I was doing, how I was doing. They would not because of what they suspected. Because of what they knew. They knew me. And because I brought him — because I *wanted* to bring him — I'd betrayed both of us to all of them.

She said, 'Does it bother you?'

'What?'

She tapped her hand on my chest as if tapping my heart. 'Most people trust what they see is true. They don't stop long enough to see what lies beneath.'

'What do you see?'

'I see what it is you want,' she said and looked up at me, 'and I see such pain.'

As we danced, I could have told Iris that the connection I felt with Morgan was similar to the connection I felt with her. I could have told Iris the nature of my true feelings for Morgan. And I could have even told her that because of these feelings, most of the time he and I spent together was carried out in the dark, lest our associations be pointed out and ridiculed. But it was her wedding night; all this could wait for a better time. Then again, I couldn't be sure there ever would be a better time.

The day had started unblemished but now large, thick clouds moved over like smoke from a bushfire — the moonlight showed the clouds encroaching. I walked back to the house. As I neared, it grew as if it'd always been waiting to crush me. Its personality expressed more than roof, walls, window. I trod with care along the length of the driveway. I placed my hand over the door handle. I wasn't sure what would greet me inside. Pressed my cheek against the grain. Closed my eyes. A rumble of thunder, this time closer.

Inside, my childhood bedroom seemed ransacked by a burglar, one who on finding nothing of value had thrown everything across the floor. I made my way into the sitting room, where the fire was lit, fresh, in anticipation of the cool change. Morgan stood in the middle of it all.

'There's a storm coming,' he said.

'Thought I'd get inside before the lightning turned me to glass.'

'I want to say something to you. I re-read your letters while you were out.'

'And?'

'And I'm having a really bad time.'

'Because of my letters?'

'Not because of your letters.'

'Because of coming here?'

'I keep going over and over — just a few things. Important things. They keep coming back to me.'

'What things?'

'Things, Christopher,' he stressed, 'memories — feelings from memories. When you can't remember things but you feel them. Like an imprint on my soul. A past place.' His shoulders rolled like two firm boulders rotating in discomfort under the earth — stone caps blocking the flow of magma deeper within.

I waited for the expected eruption. I was the voiceless sea. And as a voiceless sea surrounding Marlo, I consumed Morgan from all angles; my lapping waves wore down his natural features. I waited, ready to sizzle and spit back his expulsions in steamy puffs of boiling liquid. He was silent.

'What feelings, Morgan?'

'Boys,' he said, 'and girls. And houses, homes, clubs, cafés, bars, gardens. Who I have been and chosen to be and told to be and wanted to be in all those places. And I thought I was certain of myself. You brought me here and I had to reveal myself. Who I am and where I come from has always been on show for everyone to guess at, to make a judgement about. But never — until now — has what I keep inside been exposed. It makes me feel so shame-filled, because now these people have two reasons to shun and despise me. I've had enough of feeling shame, and I'm beyond letting others put shame into me.'

I had a sudden vision of pinning his body to the ground, ripping the clothes from him. Consuming him.

'When we were discovered in that alley at the zoo. When you went through my travel case — five minutes I was gone. Five minutes. But that's all it takes, isn't it?'

The storm outside had set in, so we had to raise our voices.

'I don't know what you want me to do.'

He replied, as if the weather itself, 'I thought, after everything, you'd let me show you.'

I looked at the floor, my shoes.

'I can't get away from myself,' he said, 'can't just forget.' He pointed at me, then at himself. 'There might be things that separate us, but we are the same in here.' His heart. 'I just wanted something normal.' He moved towards me with his fist raised in the air. 'But how can I feel normal when all these people tell me that I will never belong?'

Nothing more except the weather occurred, gusting. So I closed the windows. The waves tossed in the same ugly wind on the other side of the glass. Rain fell. Morgan shouted, but I couldn't hear him. Neither of us would be here in the morning because we'd be blown over in the storm. There was nothing to do but get into bed. I lay with eyes open, listened out for the crack of lightning shooting down into my heart. Once we were in bed, there was enough light in the room to make out the shape of his body across from me. It flickered when the lightning struck. My neck was tight, my right shoulder pinched from the position I'd slept in the previous night. At some stage, Morgan rolled over, close. I pretended sleep. He whispered. He pulled my body on top of his own. His lips prepared my mouth for a specific use. His palms asserted themselves on my shoulders and guided me towards his crotch. I tried to defy his hands, which now pressed down on the top of my head.

We returned to the city. The train, like purgatory, dragged us through a pathetic landscape, into growing suburbia. At the station, we gathered our things in silence. We disembarked, looked at each other, and shook hands. His hand was so warm I wanted to kiss it.

Once home, in my home, his absence wandered through the hallways. I saw him on the couch. I saw him in my bed. I saw him in the kitchen. I hadn't seen or heard from Morgan for two or three weeks. I began expecting to never see him again. A toxic, exotic blend of shame suffocated me. Sitting on my hands was about all I could do. I attempted to send a letter to him but got no reply; I got no reply because I did not send the letter at all. I did not finish the letter. I sat on my bed with the duvet over my legs. Used a hardcover book to compose my attempts, but threw away the pencil I was using. Screwed up the paper, unscrewed it, and flattened it back out. Creased. Crevassed. Crumpled. Scrunched it again, un-scrunched. Hit my forehead with the book. I tore my failed letter into small pieces and fluttered them out the open window, where they floated down into a great daisy shrub sitting under the bedroom bay window. I rested my arms on the window ledge. A bright afternoon stretched overhead. Light breeze smelled of cut grass. And, of course, a butterfly, which flicked down and landed on a piece of torn paper, like a dumb fish to a well-made fly sitting on top of the water.

When I'd first written to him, I'd been so caught up by whether we might end up in prison. Now, without him, I'd spend any day in prison if it meant I'd hear from him. I withdrew from where I was perched and shuttered the window. I fell back on my bed. Rolled onto my stomach, head turned to the side, to the door. It was open, wide. Anyone could pick the pieces of the torn letter and put it back together.

> At first, I hid your letters. Between the
> mattress of my bed and the frame that
> held it up, letters you had sent. One or
> two could have been missing, lost forever.
> Then I burnt them. Sorry I didn't take
> better care of them. The marks your pencil,
> sometimes pen, made in the paper curled
> round and round and round each other.

Your address was written neat in block
letters on the back of each envelope, as if
you wanted me to focus on it. Never had I
been that far out from my suburb …

Your house could be on a hill. A yellow-
mustard brick place set on an angle within
a large block of land. A garden of mixed
vegetation growing where a winding
driveway of blue gravel did not cut
through. In the early evening, gold light
from the three windows that faced the
front of the property; the light rested on
long patterns over the hedges and trees but
did not reach me.

Perhaps one day when I was long dead, a future
relative loosely connected to me would peer into
Melbourne's history, pore over myriad recordings, and
find not one nice word written about me and my kind,
but a thousand, and more, nasty lies. The *arkhé* of the
pervert. I wanted to lick the print from the paper, wanted
to spit it out into the gutter, because its truth remained
unsavoury.

The alcohol I drank seemed to do more than just
flow through me; it seeped past the boundaries of my
veins and arteries, poisoning my organs and fatty tissue.
I got lost in that numb feeling but it meant that for a

short time I no longer felt the mære sitting on my chest. I could have fallen into the river that cut Melbourne in north and south and I would not have hit the surface but floated above it, my alcohol-induced confidence enough to suspend me. Sometimes it was so strong that I thought about how it'd be to smash the bottle-green glass and take a slice across my forearm. It would not be the veins that controlled how the blood came out from me, no: I'd decide where, when, and I'd control and I'd determine that sweet-metallic liquid. From me. Of course, I'd have these thoughts at night only to wake in the morning with a head heavier than I cared to carry and I'd run my fingers, tingling, over my skin to find it still intact.

I returned to my old rhythm, the one I had made for myself when I first moved to the city. Its familiarity soothed: wake, get up, wash, garage, grease, gears, go home, eat, wash, sleep, repeat. Working at the mechanics was some kind of balm, soothing for its numbing effect. I'd lose myself in the clank, the cleaning up of other people's grease. I spoke to Nash about the finer details of this or that part of a vehicle's motor: naming the malfunctioning parts served as a lullaby. A monotonous distraction.

When I got home, I stripped naked. Ran a bath, hot and steamy. Retrieved a bottle of merlot from the dining-room cabinet and poured a glass. I sank into the water. Above me, orbital satellites — Da, Iris, Giacomo, Kings, Ma, Jimmy, Nash, and Morgan. I soaped up the face washer, scrubbed against my neck and shoulders, under my armpits and over my chest. Steam twisted upward; I poked my finger into its curls, which broke and dissolved. To take a bath was to soak in your own filth and remind yourself of who you truly were. But I was not in the water or anywhere else in the room. Plain-white walls, clean canvases ready to be primed with the blood of a suicide. I could have gotten so drunk that I passed out and drowned. I tossed the wine glass at the wall.

Fuck.

Fuck it.

Fuck it all.

Try to visit the Gardens without preying. No control. There was no control. I first noticed it at school, cheating on arithmetic tests by looking over at Kings, wanting both his answers and to taste his sweat. On hot Fridays at the end of term when smoke from fires loomed. Sweat everywhere on my skin, staining patches of my sky-blue T-shirt. On my way home, walking on the dirt path, and beside me Kings. *Kings*. It was a momentary infatuation long, long ago, but as a formative memory it expressed something unspeakable. It took hold of me as Giacomo entered my life; that sensitive, masculine prisoner of war swung through my world when everyone thought the world would end. It didn't. But felt as if it was. And he crashed into me, open. All the men I'd been with, and now just me sitting alone in the bathtub with the steam rising, foggy to see.

I reckoned the rough trade went by at the beat, hands shoved deep in their pockets, suspicious eyes and rustling feet. The damned current of life flowed through them, as through me, and through all the guys behind me and after me. Black silhouettes were waiting. The same ones Morgan had told me about from his childhood game. They waited. Out front, they checked their watches for the time. Waited and thought about leaving. I wondered if Morgan was drunk … or getting as drunk as me. I wondered if he was thinking about those black silhouettes, too. I wondered if the one he'd told me about was me. Was I the person in the room he had no access to and the figure pointing a gun at him? Maybe Morgan had left where he lived for the night, trundled through the darkened streets, coughed up a gorbie as it started to rain. He might have crossed the level crossing. The next train would be there. The next train would be there, soon. He could have been standing on the tracks waiting for that train to come. Soon. So he could close his eyes. So he could wait. So he could rest. Because he could wait in the pouring rain and cross on tippy-toes the slippy tracks. His chin landed on his chest and he grunted. He pissed along the side of the road, but no one would notice because of the rain and the black silhouettes snapping at his heels. Those silhouettes were coming for me, too.

I scavenged through drawers, shelves. My feet scuffed against the floor and fell dumbly away. Untethered. A light was on. I rifled in my bookshelf behind a copy of the King James, which stood slender but tall, and concealed behind it a shiny bottle of whiskey. Swallowing the whiskey, I puffed my chest, ready to pound a pansy into the earth. I slugged more whiskey, deep, and left. Swayed into the street, walked by back roads and unlit alleys, kept to the shadows. I was a shadow.

At the side entry to the Botanic Gardens my jacket caught a wire, tore a neat hole in the material. I tripped on mulch, smelled dank earth as I helped myself up. Prowled onto the path. The Gardens increased in size, or perhaps it was my own senses inflating. In the bogs, I kicked in each of the cubicle doors. Yelled at the space inside: 'Jacqui.' The quean was nowhere. At the basin, I ran the tap, rinsed my face. Myself in the mirror. What do other men see each time they look? Under the flickering electric light, I saw what Morgan must have seen and what Iris told me she had seen: the things I want, the things I cannot have, and such pain. I punched the glass. Nursed my hand, brought it close to my stomach. There was no one to help me bandage it. What other men saw each time they looked: filth; lust; pervert; skin; criminal; company.

A voice, gravelly and common, sounded behind me. It said something that I didn't catch, but it didn't matter because the tenor of his voice — low, vibrating — excited.

It was inside me. Its effect similar to when I'd been in the guts of that widgie's car and Nash had rapped on its metal, making it rattle all round my head. The mirror trembled, and I lost sight of my own conscious face.

He suggested we leave; I could not see any of his features, only the dark shape of his body.

I considered the broken mirror and my throbbing hand. I considered, too, Jacqui's words from the first time we met. But my thoughts lacked the clarity of a sober mind. I fell in line behind him; he kept checking back at me over his shoulder, just as Jacqui had done. Big shoulders under his trench coat. Muscles ran up his neck and protruded as he turned his head; I wanted to reach out and stroke them. The bulge diminished when he looked back ahead, but the memory of his strength remained. Quicken. Moonlight filled some of the Gardens — no one else there. If something happened to you, how long would it be before someone found you? How would they find you?

No one knew I was there.

We made our way towards where I had once walked with Millie. Soon the shrubs would conceal us. Up, up, up the hill, until we reached the top. It was windy and when I tried to speak, my words were blown away. He grabbed my arms and shoved me under a giant fig tree. It was then that a second man stepped forward from out of nowhere.

'No,' I swallowed.

Both men were tall. The second swayed under the moonlight flickering through the leaves. He came forward until he was right in front of me.

'I've changed my mind.' My voice broke.

The same head, same shoulders, intercepted my vision. A calloused hand clamped my mouth. A crotch pressed my arse. A forearm tightened round my throat. Instead of turning me around and pulling down my jeans, the first man punched me in the stomach. The man holding me released me and I fell, my forehead hitting the ground. One of them lifted me by my jacket while the other laid his steelcap boot into my ribs; I coughed. Kicks jolted me from side to side, as if I were a child being rocked to sleep. I crawled. Stood. My eyes stung from the blood that had seeped into them. I used the decline of the hill as a guide. I ran through garden beds. I made my way down. I didn't care if they followed: as long as I made it to the bogs, I'd have a better chance of someone finding me under the electric light. I stumbled on my feet. Where was Jacqui? The dumb nance wasn't fixing her dumb face, tapping her finger at the corners of her lips in the toilet's mirror. On my cheek, dark blood wound into another trail and, conjoined, they twisted further away. Pain shrank my body, down, then laid me across the tiled floor. Beside me were the shards of glass from the mirror my fist had shattered when I'd first arrived. I could use the shards to finish off the job those two men had started.

My thoughts were moving wildly. What did all this matter then? The police, the pain. Capture. Disease. You deserve this, don't you? Even if you didn't ask to be born in Marlo? Even if you didn't ask for Ma to die? Even if you didn't want Jimmy's gentle hand against your nervous lips? Even if you didn't trip Morgan — or did he trip on you? Travel all you like along a straight trajectory, you could not prevent the world from cutting you short. There were structures in place, and if you did not dovetail into these you fell, discarded, on the workroom floor. Try making your way through the onslaught of margery, nance, and ponce. Try to pretend: *she'd make a wondrous wife!* Just try. Just navigate: your speech, your body, your eyes. Just hide in the company of those who always assume you are not what you know you are. Always look in the opposite direction.

I looked from the broken glass to the toilet's door. There had to be a better way, out there in the world beyond the Gardens. Crisp air stung my wounds. Each step provoked intense pain from my groin into the middle of my chest. Through the side exit, I passed a streetwalker who ignored me. I'd rather take the tram, the train, a taxi — anything quicker (I could be bleeding out). But my face, the blood: me. Just me. I was a risk. They'd know. They would all know. If I were caught I'd end up in jail and never see Morgan again. I sat on the kerb to catch my breath, to vomit.

At home, I found the nailbrush in the cupboard

under the vanity in my bathroom and then slid into the bathtub's water, which had been sitting there since earlier. Water grey, cold. I gasped. My smashed wine glass reminded me of how I got here. When I reached round to wash my back, a sharp pain through my rib cage stopped me. Water splashed up and over the edge of the tub onto the tiled floor. I could have cried, I could have screamed. I gave my body to the shape of the tub, too tired to move.

On my cheek, a dark wound. A slash above my eyebrow. Yellow-and-green-mottled skin. *You'd been caught. Found out. Those two men knew why you were there. You played their game.* His hands still clasped my biceps — so much stronger than me, shoving me to where he wanted me. Under his control. He could have lowered me into the lake, my head submerged, and I'd have no choice but to breathe in a lungful. Moonlight flickering over my bloated face.

At the garage, Nash chuckled when he saw how I looked. 'Y'missus did a number on you, Chrissy.'

I made sure my shoulder clipped his as I walked by him. I remained quiet because I didn't need a deep voice, didn't need to be part of a group, or have a hard, tough, rough body: men like that were the kinds of men who hid in bushes and bashed men like me.

'Yer missed a spot, mate.' One lad stood behind me;

a few others lounged about nearby, like vultures waiting for a carcass.

I looked where he was pointing. 'There's nothing.'

'Might be nothin' there,' the lad said, 'but can't say the same fer y'face.'

'Get fucked.' I went back to sweeping.

The lad punched my shoulder, harder than a laddish way.

We faced each other.

He held out a bottle of slick black oil. Tipped it so a shiny ribbon poured and spread out over the concrete. 'Since we got a woman here,' he said, 'may as well get her to work cleanin' up the joint. What d'yers think, boys?'

I was not discarded on the workroom floor. I was not a margery, a nance, a ponce. I no longer wanted to navigate my speech or body or eyes. These men knew what I was and would no longer look in the opposite direction.

'Go on, boys,' I said.

They *ooooo*-ed and one of them said, 'He's got a tongue.'

'Go on, boys,' I yelled and swiped a tool case from the workbench. 'G'on!'

None of them moved; they were silent and staring. I spat on the ground and left the garage.

I returned home no more than an hour after I'd left. I collapsed on the bed, still fully dressed. Exhausted of myself and of the world. Heavy. I needed a bath, to wash.

I needed to close my eyes against the steam. To smell my clean skin and feel the warmth of the water against me.

A knock at my front door echoed down the hall.

Tired of the outside world's interruptions I whispered, 'Fuck off,' into the mattress.

A louder knock.

I said, 'Fuck off,' louder. This time they'd hear it. And perhaps they did, perhaps they didn't. The reply from the front door was not a knock but a rattle. I got on my hands and knees, waited. Nothing. Another rattle confirmed that whoever was behind the door was, indeed, inserting a key into the lock. I wanted to scream. The door unlocked. The door handle turned. I got up and stood in the hall, staring down to where the front door opened.

'Morgan?'

He closed the door behind him. 'I still have the spare key.' He placed it on the hall stand. 'Your face,' he said.

'Why are you here?'

He placed one palm on the side of my face. 'I wanted to.' He used his other hand to assess a wound above my eyes. 'I was beginning to think you were a hallucination. I had to prove to myself you really existed.'

'I don't think I deserve you,' I said.

'Whether or not you deserve me is not your choice. I'm not yours.' He dropped his arms, as if letting go of some weight from within him. He was not touching any part of me. 'I am not anybody's.'

A car backfiring outside broke between us.

He leant his shoulder against the wall, crossed his arms over his chest. I leant my back against the opposite wall, my hands dug into my pockets.

'Everything we do is by the cover of darkness,' he said.

'Or in out-of-the-way side streets.'

'Or godforsaken garden beds.' He paused. 'I'm sick of it.' He stared, soft eyes, at me. 'I'm not yours and I'm not asking you to be mine.'

'Neither am I, Morgan. I'm just asking you to stick around.'

AUTHOR'S NOTE

In the 'Introduction' of the 1971 printing of *Homosexual: oppression and liberation*, Dennis Altman contends that 'the homosexual in literature has generally been a tragic figure [and] most attempts to see homosexuality in a broader context have tended to reinforce social opprobrium and homosexual misery' (2012). Altman challenges the tradition of tragedy in queer literature. The tradition of tragedy means the way, for example, that homosexual characters aren't afforded the same happiness heterosexual characters are and that homosexual characters often meet an untimely, lonely death (Woods 1998).

The term 'homosexuality', as defined in 'Homosexuality and Virility' by Régis Revenin, is the 'set of affective, amorous, cultural, social, and/or sexual relations between men, whether or not [men] define themselves as homosexual, whether they have exclusively or occasionally homosexual relations' (2016). This definition includes people who do and who do not identify as homosexual, which is poignant and useful: this novel is set during a time when homosexuality was seen as a medical condition rather than as an identity. In other words, men who had sex with men, or at least were attracted to other men, may not have identified as any kind of '-sexual', despite their sexual behaviours or affections.

Pathologised homosexuality has a notorious history and is still punishable in many countries in 2022, even by death. According to Revenin, this is largely because of religious beliefs that homosexuality goes 'against divine law' and that homosexuals 'defy nature [...] the identity of the sodomite, then, is constituted by the wrong done to natural law' (2016). These religious beliefs were often enforced on the original inhabitants of colonised lands.

It is to anti-happiness depictions such as this that Altman dedicates much space in *Homosexual*, principally to how male homosexuality is mis/represented in society and how gay liberation movements have sought to overcome this. Altman uses bountiful examples from fiction, TV, stage, and media. He argues that the gay liberation movements were, in part, fighting to reverse the tradition of homosexual tragedy. This is likely because gay liberation movements had global activist appeal — put simply: 'gay men come from all classes, belong to all religions, are found in all forms of human settlements, work places and environments' (Robinson 2006). It's not just that male homosexuality has been ever-present, but rather that it is because of its ever-presence that it has had myriad mis/representations within law, religion, art, and, importantly for this novel, writing (Woods 1998).

Marlo began as an exploration of mid-century representations of male homosexuality. It is set sometime during the early 1950s. My reasons for choosing this period are that homosexuality was under intense scrutiny during this time, homosexuality was not represented favourably during this time, and there's a gap in what's known about male homosexual life during mid-century Australia, for a number of reasons.

The first is that male homosexuals living in mid-century Australia came to the attention of the Australian Intelligence Security Organisation (ASIO), which was during this period only being set up (Horner 2015). Aside from its initial purpose of tracking communist spies, ASIO was actively doing the same kind of spy work on 'known male homosexuals' (Horner 2015; Willett 1997). This was because homosexuality was seen to pose a threat to nationhood (Willett 1997).

Second, in such a society, homosexuals didn't face the same pressures or encouragement they do today 'to declare their sexuality publicly' (Robinson 2006); in fact, doing so could very well land you in prison. Robinson argues that male homosexuals of the 1940s and 1950s were, instead, 'brought out', meaning the often clandestine process by which they were initiated into 'social and/or sexual practices by a more experienced [gay] person' (2006). In other words, gay men may have encountered another gay person almost by accident, such as by unknowingly visiting a beat (e.g. a park or public toilet where men meet other men for sex). And through their encounter they would learn how to navigate their sexuality in a world that sought to cure homosexuality.

And finally, by the 1950s 'the attention paid to the problem of homosexuality by various professions and disciplines was increasing in Australia' (Willett 1997). Willett argues that while 'parliaments, medical journals, the universities, government inquiries and government departments all had something to say during this decade' (including what ASIO kept secret), what was being discussed by such institutions was 'taking place well away from the public gaze' (1997). Instead, the public were presented with newspaper articles lambasting homosexuality, and this kind of writing set the tone for many people on how they should consider and treat someone suspected of being homosexual (religiosity aside). Such messages that persisted include this from the *Telegraph* (Brisbane, 5 August 1941, p. 8):

> 'This is a particularly filthy and revolting thing. [The accused's] signed statement contains in detail this grossest form of unnatural act. He is a sexual pervert,' said

Mr. J. A. Sheehy, Crown Prosecutor, in the
Criminal Court to-day, when he presented
an indictment against [the accused], who
was charged that on June 12, at Brisbane,
he had carnal knowledge of a male person.
In sentencing [the accused] to four years'
imprisonment, Mr. Justice E. A. Douglas
said it was a dreadful case. 'I think you are
a man who is a danger to the community,
especially young boys.'

And from the *Singleton Argus* (NSW, 5 January 1949, p. 2):

Since the Vice Squad started its drive
against the growing menace of sex perverts
three weeks ago, 20 perverts ranging in age
from 23 to 58 have been detained.

Articles like this pathologised homosexuality by referring
to a man as a 'sexual pervert', as in abnormally developed,
meaning that homosexuality became a medical condition. The articles often included advice from medical
professionals, like this from Dr J. Cooper Booth, who
was the director of the NSW venereal-disease division
(*Singleton Argus*, 5 January 1949, p.2):

The homosexual exists, and has always
existed. Medical opinion is that he should

be harassed as little as possible — provided
he does not offend against the established
systems of society.

'Surveillance, silencing, fear, and victimisation' were thus
the hallmarks of 1950s Australia, and it was a period in
which sentiment from governing bodies towards homosexuality in particular was hostile (Willett 1997). The
1950s saw a dramatic increase in how many men were
convicted in Australia for 'unnatural offences': in 1938
there were 50 convictions, which doubled in 1941, and
peaked at 350 convictions for homosexuality in 1958,
with more than 3,000 people being convicted between
1945 and 1960 in Australia for 'unnatural offences'
(Willett 1997). This is likely a contributing factor to
there being very little public archival material. Willett
(1997) argues that such 'mobilisation against homosexuality' meant many men who were homosexual were

subjected to the relentless pressure of
a society that neither understands nor
approves of their kind ... this is reflected
in a debilitating day-to-day fear: the
disapproval of family and friends; of being
beaten up by the men they meet in bars; of
blackmail; of police entrapment; of arrest,
exposure, infamy, and disgrace.

Male homosexuals were considerably constrained by how they could express their identities, such as

> in only being able to kiss goodnight if the
> street was dark enough; only being able
> to hold hands in cinemas and in the car if
> their touching was out of the line of sight;
> in searching for a flat where the windows
> were not open to on-lookers who might
> see them forget themselves for a moment
> and a kiss (Willett 1997).

The medicalisation of homosexuality during the 1940s and 1950s focused on cure rather than trying to understand the behaviour of male homosexuality. This meant many medical and health professionals could not comprehend male homosexuality as equally valid an identity as heterosexuality — or even as an identity at all. Sexuality was seen as behavioural, and therefore fell into 'natural' and 'unnatural' categories, and because homosexuality was seen as 'unnatural' behaviour, the material about homosexuality that became today's archival material refers only to it in terms of disgust, cure, menace. There is no holistic account of the lived experiences of male homosexuals in the 1940s and 1950s.

Including the character of Morgan in the narrative as an Indigenous man — who is subject to a suite of laws collectively called the 'white Australia policy' — further questions what lived experiences are excluded from the predominantly white archival record.

All of which means that there's a gap in what we today can know and understand about how life was lived as a male homosexual under societal scrutiny and persecution during mid-century Australia. Such lives must largely be inferred. This is the task of the historical novel.

REFERENCES

Altman, D 2012, *Homosexual: oppression and liberation*, University of Queensland Press, Brisbane.

Horner, D 2015, *The Spy Catchers: the official history of ASIO, 1949–1963*, Allen & Unwin, Crows Nest.

Revenin, R 2016, 'Homosexuality and Virility', in Corbin, A, Courtine, J & Vigarello, G (eds), *A History of Virility*, Columbia University Press, New York, pp. 362–390.

Robinson, P 2006, 'The Changing World of Gay Men, 1950–2000', thesis, RMIT University, viewed 3 June 2017, <researchbank.rmit.edu.au/eserv/rmit:6795/Robinson.pdf>

Woods, G 1998, *A History of Gay Male Literature: the male tradition*, Yale University Press, New Haven.

Willett, G 1997, 'The Darkest Decade: homophobia in 1950s Australia', *Australian Historical Studies*, vol. 27, no. 109, pp. 120–132.

ACKNOWLEDGEMENTS

Dino Hodge, Peter Waples-Crowe, Marika Webb-Pullman, Dr Ruth McIver, Grace Heifetz, Dr Graham Willett, Wolfram-Jaymes Keesing, and the Australian Queer Archives. Special thanks to Dr Olga Lorenzo.

Marlo is set during a time when the Traditional Custodians of the place we call Australia were not recognised. This story takes place on the unceded and sovereign Country of the Gunaikurnai people and the Kulin Nations.

The following images have been reproduced from the State Library Victoria collection: on the cover, Image H87.271/91, 'Foundation Day, 1930'; on p. 12, Image H2008.11/634, 'Streetscenes, Melbourne, Vic.', 1950, Mark Strizic; on p. 30, Image H2009.143/99, 'Botanical Gardens, Melbourne', c. 1920–1960, Carl Reinhold Hartmann; on p. 46, Image H92.20/3395, 'Capitol House Swanston Street Melbourne designed by Walter Burley Griffin', 1950, Lyle Fowler; and, on p. 105,